Tennis Term at
TREBIZON

Tennis Term at TREBIZON

ANNE DIGBY

EGMONT

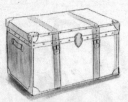

EGMONT

We bring stories to life

Tennis Term at Trebizon
First published by Granada Publishing Ltd 1981
This edition published 2016
by Egmont UK Limited
The Yellow Building, 1 Nicholas Road, London W11 4AN

Text copyright © 1981 Anne Digby
Illustrations copyright © 2016 Lucy Truman

The right of Anne Digby to be identified as the author of
the work has been asserted by her in accordance with the
Copyright, Designs and Patents Act 1988.

ISBN 978 1 4052 8068 6

www.egmont.co.uk

Typeset in Goudy Old Style by Avon DataSet Ltd, Bidford on Avon,
Warwickshire
Printed and bound in Great Britain by CPI Group

Stay safe online. Any website addresses listed in this book are correct
at the time of going to print. However, Egmont is not responsible
for content hosted by third parties.

Please be aware that online content can be subject to change and websites can
contain content that is unsuitable for children. We advise that all children are
supervised when using the internet.

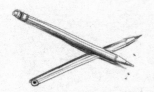

CONTENTS

For Melanie

ONE
An Eye-Opening Dress

In Rebecca Mason's sixth term at Trebizon, two amazing hoaxes were played at school. The first one was played on Miss Welbeck and the second, on the whole school. Rebecca and her friends, Tish Anderson, Sue Murdoch and the rest of their Action Committee, were getting used to solving mysteries – but this one was really odd. It took a long time to find the answer.

It was quite a term, though, not just because of the hoaxes. Other things about that summer term lingered on in Rebecca's mind even longer.

There was Robbie . . . and the tennis . . . and the painting . . . and the fact that it was Pippa's last term. Perhaps that most of all.

Afterwards, whenever Rebecca looked at the

painting, it brought it all back to her – the tennis term – the hot red dust of the courts with the sun beating down on them and afterwards the cool, dark, spreading shade of the big cedar tree. She would see them, again, through Pippa's eyes.

'I love this tree,' the older girl told Rebecca, on the first day back. 'In fact I love Trebizon. I've been so happy here, I want my last term to be the best ever! And I want this –' she touched the canvas with the end of her paintbrush '– to be the best ever, too.'

'What will you do with it when it's finished?' asked Rebecca shyly.

Rebecca had unpacked and eaten tea and changed into her blue tracksuit. Now, tennis racket in hand, she was on her way to south courts. But she could see that nobody had arrived there yet and so she'd stopped to talk to Pippa, while keeping an eye on the tennis courts.

Pippa Fellowes-Walker was never too busy to talk to her, even though she was in the Upper Sixth and a prefect. She was also in Trebizon's first tennis team, editor of the school's superb magazine, *The Trebizon Journal*, and a gifted artist as well.

She'd set up her easel within sight of the school's ancient cedar tree. The tree was a most beautiful thing, and she had lightly worked it in on the canvas with, beyond, a glimpse of the main school building, an eighteenth-century manor house of mellow stone that always seemed to reflect a soft, warm light.

It looked like the beginnings of a lovely picture.

'If it works,' said Pippa, 'it's going to be the cover of my last *Journal*. I like the composition, but it lacks something at the moment.'

Rebecca watched her working, in silence. She felt a sudden desire to try and write something for *The Journal* this term! Something really good, though she didn't know what. She also decided that she wanted Pippa's wish to come true, too – a marvellous last term at Trebizon, with nothing to spoil it. Yes, she wanted that very much for Pippa – who wouldn't?

She carried on watching, from time to time squinting towards the tennis courts, which were still deserted.

'Who are you playing with?' asked Pippa. 'You're going to miss Josselyn. So's the team.'

'I know,' sighed Rebecca. Why did Joss Vining, who was in Rebecca's form and the best player in the Middle School, if not the whole of Trebizon, have to go off to California for a year? Rebecca needed strong competition now – and how many team members would have the time to play with her regularly the way Joss did? It was maddening.

'I'll play with you when I can,' said Pippa. 'But with A Levels this term it's going to take me all my time to manage team practices and matches. You know what, Rebecca,' she added lightly, 'you'll just have to get into the team yourself!'

Rebecca's heart seemed to jump a bit.

'Who are you going to play with now?'

'Robbie Anderson – you know, Tish's brother. I saw him on the train and he said he'd try and get away from Garth after tea.' Rebecca gazed towards the courts again, anxiously. 'Doesn't look as though he can make it.'

'Pity,' said Pippa. 'He's good. How did you get on in the holidays? With the sponsorship? Were the people you stayed with nice?'

'Very!' nodded Rebecca. Her parents were in Saudi Arabia and a Greek family had looked after her in London while she took part in some junior tennis competitions. It had been fun. 'Very nice. And do you know what? Yesterday, they took me to that big store in Knightsbridge and let me choose a new party dress to bring back to school! It's a model, I think. They *bought* it for me!'

'I hope you get some parties then!' laughed Pippa. 'If you don't there's always Commem. I'll be over at Court later – the Barringtons are going out – you can show it to me.'

Pippa loved clothes.

She looked across to the empty courts and suddenly put her brush down.

'Look, what's happening about this tennis? Would you like me to give you a game?'

'No, honestly, Pippa –' began Rebecca.

She spun round as she heard a bicycle bell behind her. Robbie was riding over the grass! His tennis racket was clipped to his bike.

'Hallo! I've been over to the boarding house looking for you!'

'Oh – I thought we said the courts –' laughed Rebecca in relief.

'And I thought you meant Court!' said Robbie. 'Very confusing. Come on, then!'

Pippa smiled and picked up her brush again.

It was good practice playing with Robbie. He played a very strong game.

But afterwards it was rather like talking to Pippa all over again.

'I'll try and get over when I can, Rebeck.' He ran a hand through his hair, which was black and curly like his sister's. 'I did enjoy it. The trouble is I've got GCSEs this term and I'm in the Garth team, which means an hour's practice every day. You know, they ought to put you in the Trebizon team! If you're in, you're playing against good people all the time and everything's organised for you. If you're not, well you just have to fix up things for yourself as best you can and the strong players are always booked up because they're in the team. So that as they get better, you get worse. It's a vicious circle. Not fair, really.'

'Joss always found time to play with me,' said Rebecca in a small voice. 'I suppose being in the same form it was easy to fix it up quickly when we felt like it.'

'And it was winter and there were no team practices and Joss is a fanatic!' laughed Robbie.

Then, seeing Rebecca's woebegone face, he became serious.

'It's obvious. You've *got* to get yourself into the team!'

'How?' asked Rebecca. 'I just haven't got the experience. I know I've had county coaching and everything –'

'And you should have had it years ago. But you're a natural, Rebecca! Surely they can see that? Maybe you *can* get into the team. Three strong players left last year and Joss Vining's on this American thing –'

It was an electrifying thought.

'Please help me, Robbie,' Rebecca begged. 'I want to get into the team!'

He grinned at her.

'I'm free on Sunday,' he said. 'Let's make an afternoon of it. Let's work on your serve. When it comes to girls' tennis, a big serve always gives you an edge.'

'Thanks, Robbie!'

He cycled away and Rebecca walked slowly back to Court House, loitering and watching the sun go down over by Trebizon Bay, and daydreaming about the possibilities.

'Try it on!' shrieked Tish.

'Come on, Rebecca, don't keep us in suspense!' said Sue.

Rebecca had got back to the boarding house to find that her two room-mates had found her new party outfit hanging in the clothes cupboard and pounced on it. Tish was holding it up –

'Come *on*!'

'I'm all hot and sticky after playing tennis with your brother,' protested Rebecca, laughing. 'He just about ran me into the ground!'

Tish bundled the dress into Rebecca's arms and started to push her out of the room. 'Go and have a shower then.'

'All right,' giggled Rebecca, quite excited now as she put the soft blue material against her cheek. 'I'm going, I'm going!'

When she returned a few minutes later, they were all waiting for her in the corridor. Tish and Sue, of course, and the other three from next door.

'Rebecca!' exclaimed Margot Lawrence.

'You look so slim!' wailed Elf – Sally Elphinstone. 'And grown-up!'

Mara Leonodis just gazed at Rebecca, speechless. The dress was a wonderful shimmer of blue with white fringes round the bottom of the skirt. A matching blue stole, very long with more white fringes, was swathed around Rebecca's shoulders.

The Greek girl walked up to Rebecca and touched the stole.

'Rebecca, you look sensational!' she said.

'Wasn't it kind of Mr and Mrs Papademas?'

sighed Rebecca. It was thanks to Mara's father that Rebecca had got the tennis sponsorship and the Papademas family were old friends of his.

'I am *jealous*!' laughed Mara. 'I shall go and stay with Aunty Papademas next holidays, just see if I don't.'

The friends insisted on showing Rebecca off to the other Third Years in the rooms across the corridor – Jane and Jenny and Elizabeth and the two Annes – and Aba. It was good to see Aba back from Nigeria after her missed term. Then they paraded their fashion model into the Common Room and drew more exclamations from some of the older girls.

Only Margaret Exton was churlish.

'You're only thirteen, you don't need a dress like that.'

'I'll be fourteen this summer!' said Rebecca.

Tish stuck her tongue out at the Fourth Year girl.

Suddenly a voice called out from the corridor:

'It's bedtime, you lot.'

It was Pippa! She was on duty and she'd said she'd be coming over to Court House.

The others pushed Rebecca out into the corridor – 'Come on, show Pippa!'

'Rebecca!'

The Upper Sixth girl stared at her.

'It – it's the outfit, Pippa. They made me put it on!' Rebecca smiled. 'You said you wanted to see it –'

Pippa closed her eyes and then opened them, wide.

'Doesn't she look terrific?' asked Sue. 'She never thought she'd own anything like this!'

'You looked quite startled, Pippa,' observed Tish.

Pippa gave a gentle smile.

'Not just startled. Stunned! Do you know, I didn't recognise you? But it suits you – it suits you perfectly. Yes, Rebecca. I must say I like your taste.'

'All I need now,' said Rebecca, wryly, 'is a chance to wear it.'

'Roll on Commem,' said Pippa, lightly. 'It'll be perfect for that. Mind you look after it till then.'

After that, Rebecca got ready for bed. Feeling a bit like Cinderella, she hung the dress and stole up in the cupboard and laid out her school uniform for the morning.

'Do you two really like it?' she asked drowsily, lying in bed later.

'Like it?' whispered Sue from across the room. 'It's a dream.'

Tish turned her head on the pillow.

'Did you see Pippa's face? She couldn't get over it. What a dress!'

She was very nearly asleep.

'Once seen, never forgotten.'

Tish was so right! And that was going to be the problem.

TWO
Rebecca in Suspense

The first fortnight of term was packed with activity, but only one thing mattered to Rebecca. Would she get into the tennis team, or wouldn't she? Her mood varied between wild optimism, if she was playing well, and hopeless despair, if she wasn't. The suspense was terrible.

The six friends discussed it endlessly.

'I'll never get in!' Rebecca would say. 'Not the first team, anyway. And that's the only one that matters this term – now we know about the Inter!'

'Of course you will!'

'Della and Kate and Pippa are definites – they were in the team last year. But the other three places are wide open!'

'They'll put you in!'

'Have you seen Alison playing in the trials?' Rebecca would say. 'She's fantastic. She and Kate must have been playing all holidays.'

'Well they would do, being sisters!'

The remarkable Hissup sisters, Joanna had been the school's Head of Games the previous year and now Kate was. The youngest Hissup, Alison, was in Court House, a Fifth Year, and she was also very good at games – any games.

'Well,' Sue or somebody would say, gripped by cold realism, 'that still leaves two places wide open.'

'And what about Jilly Good? She's so tall! Seen her at the net?'

'Oh, all right then. But that still leaves *one* place.'

The friends, drinking cocoa and eating digestive biscuits late in the evening, in the kitchen at Court House, would go over the same ground, again and again.

They all wanted Rebecca to get in the team. So did Robbie. So did Mrs Ericson, the county coach. Miss Willis, who was in charge of games, would certainly have liked to see her in, if possible.

The one person who was lukewarm was Miss Darling.

'I would like to welcome a new member of staff,'

announced Miss Welbeck, the principal, at Assembly on the first morning of term. 'Miss Darling.'

'Doesn't look much of a darling to me,' mouthed Tish, to Rebecca.

'Miss Darling is joining the games staff and will be taking some of the load off Miss Willis's shoulders this term,' continued the Principal. 'She has devoted her life to tennis. She'll have sole responsibility for senior tennis and will be in charge of tennis coaching throughout the school. As a first priority she'll be organising trials and in due course selecting the senior teams for this season, in consultation with Kate Hissup, our Head of Games. The selection of the First Six is of especial importance because at Miss Darling's suggestion we have, for the first time, entered Trebizon for the inter-schools tennis cup. Now that we have a full-time tennis coach, and we're exceedingly lucky to have secured her services, we hope and expect that under her expert guidance we shall acquit ourselves well in this important championship.'

Naturally all this had an electrifying effect on Rebecca, and her rather dream-like ambition of getting into the school team took on a new edge.

It seemed that the tennis team had to be decided

at the latest by the beginning of May, which was a fortnight away, as the first round matches in the cup had to be played off during the first week of May.

But, being new to the school, Miss Darling needed all of two weeks to get to know the state of tennis at Trebizon from top to bottom and who the most promising players were. She organised a lot of trials and saw Rebecca play three times during the fortnight.

Rebecca longed to know where she stood in Miss Darling's estimation but the new games teacher gave nothing away. She was a grey-haired woman with square shoulders and a very straight back, stiff as a ramrod, and she never smiled. However, she knew the game of tennis inside out and was reputed to be a brilliant coach. Having been hired to turn Trebizon into a top tennis school she had every intention of so doing.

'I'd very much like to see Rebecca Mason in the team,' Sara Willis said to her in the Staff Room one evening. 'A really tough, hard season is exactly what she needs at this stage.'

'If we get knocked out of the cup in the first round, she may not get it,' said Miss Darling dryly. 'There are quite a few girls here who could similarly benefit. Of course Rebecca's in the running. She has to be. But we have to remember we're entering a competition, not a benefit match. We have to pick the best team.'

'I could see her in at number six,' insisted Miss Willis. 'She's remarkable. And a remarkable competitor.'

'After a year, yes, remarkable,' conceded Miss Darling. 'But the lack of experience shows. I'm not sure that Eddie Burton isn't the safer bet. It's going to be a very difficult decision.'

Lady Edwina Burton was in the Lower Sixth and a prefect.

Rebecca knew nothing of this conversation, of course; she remained in suspense. There were plenty of other things going on, so she didn't spend the entire time thinking about the tennis team. Admittedly she gave up two or three surfing sessions in Trebizon Bay, which she loved and which the others were mad about, because those were the times when Robbie was able to get over from Garth College to help her with her tennis. But she found time for some athletics and enjoyed the sprinting in particular.

There was also the question of electing a new Third Year Head of Games, now that Joss had gone, and that was quite exciting.

At one stage, to her surprise, her own name was suggested, but she quickly declined. If by any chance she *did* get into the school tennis team that, together with county junior tennis activities, was going to absorb all her time and energy!

Mara wanted Tish to stand – Tish was a good middle-distance runner and in any case, didn't they all want someone from Court House to get it?

'I'll stand next term, when we start in the Fourth Year,' said Tish, with that wide smile of hers. 'That way I could do it for a whole year, instead of just a term! Anyway I'd much rather be Head of Games in the hockey terms.'

Tish was outstanding at hockey and had already played in the Second Eleven. She would have liked a say in choosing the teams. For now she hit on the idea of asking Aba to stand: Aba was a brilliant sprinter, but not particularly interested in team games. It would be the ideal time for her to have a turn at being Head of Games.

'*And* you're in Court, Aba, which is what really matters!' she told the Nigerian girl.

'Just for you, Tish!' said Aba, secretly rather delighted.

Of course, some of the Third Years in other boarding houses had other ideas and Tavistock came up with a rival candidate – Laura Wilkins, who was in form III Beta, nearly as good a sprinter as Aba and a good all-rounder as well.

The ensuing election was exciting and hard-fought, with a lot of lobbying and campaigning going on, but Aba won – by a mere seven votes!

While Court House celebrated with barbecued sausages and lemonade on the beach, Tavistock House swore they'd get their revenge in the autumn term.

Another thing that occupied Rebecca's mind was the question of writing something for this term's *Trebizon Journal* – Pippa's last issue.

Helena King, who was Third Year Magazine Officer came over from Norris House one evening and reminded them all that items must be submitted as soon as possible, to give time to select the best and hand it in to Pippa Fellowes-Walker before the magazine went to press.

Rebecca hardly needed reminding: she had noticed Pippa working away on her painting whenever the weather was fine, obviously in a hurry to get it finished. She so wanted to submit something – something really superlative; she wanted *everything* about Pippa's last term to be superlative! That, of course, was in itself a most freezing thought – and the harder she tried to think of something, the blanker her mind became.

One very exciting thing that happened in the first fortnight was that Rebecca received an invitation – she was going to have the chance to wear her new party dress, much sooner than expected!

'It's got an Exonford postmark,' said Rebecca puzzled, taking the square white envelope from the mail board. 'It feels like a card inside.'

It *was* a card, with a gold edge and gilt lettering.

'A May Day party!' she exclaimed, as the others crowded round her. 'At the sports centre in Exonford. County tennis party – and draw for Wimbledon tickets. Oh –' Her voice went up to a squeak. 'I can wear my dress!'

But Sue looked slightly disappointed.

'Oh,' she said, staring at the card and pushing her spectacles up her nose, 'you won't be able to hear me and Annie give our duo. It's the same evening.'

'So it is,' said Rebecca. 'Oh, what a shame, Sue!'

Sue had been chosen to give a violin recital with Annie Lorrimer at a May Day concert in aid of Mulberry Castle restoration funds. It was a great honour and Sue had been practising hard. Like Annie, she was one of the school's music scholars, but Annie was in the Upper Sixth – she was sharing rooms with Pippa in Parkinson House this year – a very accomplished violinist who in her last term had been made leader of the school orchestra.

'Never mind,' said Sue with a wry smile, 'you have – er – sort of – heard the pieces we're going to play.'

They all laughed because Sue had been bringing her violin back to Court House from the Music

School most evenings and playing the pieces over and over again.

'But I was dying to go to the castle!' protested Rebecca. The concert was to be held at the castle itself, in the banqueting hall if it were wet, but otherwise in the castle keep. The castle was perched high over Mulberry Cove with spectacular sea views and it belonged to the National Trust. 'Oh well, I suppose that will make room for one more in Mrs Barry's car.'

Mr Barrington was the Director of Music and would be taking Annie and some of the Upper Sixth over, while Mrs Barrington – because she was House Mistress at Court House and apt to spoil Sue – was borrowing a car to take Sue and as many friends as she could squeeze in.

'Don't expect us to feel sorry for you, Becky,' said Tish. 'It should be a smashing party. All those dishy tennis boys! And – let's see – first of May –' she caught Rebecca's eye, '– maybe you'll have something to celebrate by then.'

'Maybe, maybe not,' replied Rebecca quickly, making a face.

'Miss Darling must announce the team before then. She *must!*' exclaimed Mara, who was even more pent up than Rebecca about it, if such a thing were possible!

It was just as well for Rebecca that she had the party to take her mind off things because, in spite of Mara's protestations, Saturday the first of May arrived and Miss Darling still hadn't announced the team. And the first cup match was only days away!

It was common knowledge now that the team was all but decided. Kate Hissup and Della Thomas were going in as a first pair. Alison Hissup had leapfrogged straight into the team as second pair, with either Jilly Good or Pippa Fellowes-Walker. The other one of those two would go in as third pair with – whom? Everyone said it would be either Rebecca Mason or Lady Edwina Burton. Nobody knew which and the juniors were running a sweepstake on it over at Juniper House.

For Rebecca, the suspense was getting unbearable. What a relief to change into her new party dress and to go right away from Trebizon for a few hours, to what was bound to be an exciting and interesting party! Mrs Barrington drove her to the station.

'Do you mind getting a taxi back from the station this evening, Rebecca?' she asked. 'I'll be tied up with the group at Mulberry Castle.' Rebecca didn't mind. She loved riding in taxis! 'Are you sure you'll be warm enough tonight, with just that stole? Silly girl!'

Rebecca enjoyed the train journey to Exonford, especially as Toby, who was in her training squad and was also going to the party, got on at the next station down the line from Trebizon. The party she enjoyed even more.

It was an annual get-together organised by the county tennis officials. Its main purpose was to give all the young county prospects a chance to meet up again early in the season, because indoor training stopped in the summer, and it was also a way of saying 'thank you' to the various west country businessmen who generously sponsored junior tennis events throughout the year. There was lots of delicious food, some dancing and games, and a talk outlining some of the arrangements for the coming weeks and what the key fixtures would be. The high point of the evening was the draw for Wimbledon tickets and although Rebecca longed to be one of the lucky ones, she drew a blank.

At the end of the evening, just when Rebecca had managed to put all thought of the school team out of her mind, her coach drew her aside.

'Thank you for letting me have your results from the competitions you entered in the holidays,' said Mrs Ericson. 'You did quite creditably. You've heard we've got a little round-robin tournament coming up – that will be useful for you. As the season goes on, I'd very much like to see if we can promote you to the next squad – but that all depends, of course. You must get plenty of tennis in at school. I hear Trebizon's entered for the Inter this year. Are you in the team?'

'I–I don't know yet,' said Rebecca dully.

'I'm sure Greta Darling will put you in if she possibly can,' said Mrs Ericson. 'My, but you're lucky to have got *her*!'

Toby walked with her to the station and Rebecca wrapped her stole round her head, as a cool breeze was blowing her hair about. He cracked a few jokes on the train but the party mood had left her now. As soon as he got off at his station she started thinking about her chances all over again.

'Cheer up!' said the taxi driver, outside Trebizon Station. 'Where're you going to?'

'Court House, please,' said Rebecca. 'Up at the school.'

He peered closely at her face in some surprise

and recognised her as the girl he brought from the Bus Station sometimes on the first day of term.

'Well, I didn't recognise you in them clothes, me dear!' he exclaimed. 'You look like a princess!'

That made Rebecca's evening.

She smiled all the way along the top road, looking out at the last dark red streaks of sunset across Trebizon Bay, and was still smiling as she swept into Court House – regally, of course.

Sue and the others had got back only five minutes before and Mara was holding the typewritten message in her outstretched hand.

'It's for you, Rebecca!' she cried, rushing out of the kitchen.

'It's from Miss Dreadful,' giggled Tish excitedly, who tended to call Miss Darling by that name.

'What – what's it about?'

'It's about the tennis team!' exclaimed Sue. 'It's between you and Eddie Burton –'

'And it's going to be decided tomorrow,' finished Tish.

THREE
The Cedar Tree

Rebecca held the narrow slip of paper under the light by the coinbox phone, in the main hall of the boarding house.

Her name, *Rebecca Mason*, was handwritten at the top. The message was typed and quite brief:

Re First Tennis VI
Play-off – Edwina Burton v. Rebecca Mason
2.30 p.m. South tennis courts. Sun. 2 May
                                                    G. *Darling*

'So the rumours are true,' Rebecca said at last, taking a deep breath. 'It *is* between the two of us – for the last place in the team!'

'It's knife-edge,' said Elf. 'Must be!'

'The Dread can't make up her mind between the two of you. That's why she's been dithering so long about announcing the team!' theorised Tish. 'Silly old –'

'You're much better than Lady Eddie!' interrupted Mara. She gazed at Rebecca with liquid brown eyes. 'She is such a dull player. Backwards and forwards – backwards and forwards – that's all she does.' She clapped her hands together. 'Oh, it is going to be so exciting. You will smash her!'

They all herded into the kitchen and made coffee and talked non-stop about how Rebecca was going to thrash Lady Edwina Burton the next day . . . Pulverize her! Grind her into dust!

There wasn't much love lost between the six and the titled girl in the Lower Sixth. She'd become bossier than ever since being made a prefect this year and was definitely on the generous side when it came to giving out reprimands, lines and the like.

'Pity it's straight after Sunday lunch,' said Elf prosaically, when they'd finished with the thrashings. 'You mustn't eat a heavy meal, Rebecca.'

Rebecca had been listening to all this in silence.

'I don't expect I'll be able to eat a thing,' she confessed.

Then quite suddenly she said, 'Let's stop talking about it. How did it go for you tonight, Sue?'

The duo had gone off very well, it seemed. Sue had made one or two small mistakes, because the pieces were difficult, but Annie Lorrimer had played beautifully.

'Do you know she's in the running for master classes in Tokyo when she leaves Trebizon?' said Sue. 'With this incredible Japanese woman –'

'Not mistress classes?' laughed Margot.

'Shut up,' giggled Rebecca.

'– they have to live in total seclusion, like a closed order, and just live for music for a whole year and nothing else. Fantastic discipline! But students fight to get in her classes, from all over the world. She's really fussy who she takes . . .'

'Japan!' exclaimed Rebecca. 'Why don't you try for that one day, Sue?'

'You deaf?' asked Tish. 'She said she's *really fussy* who she takes.'

They all laughed.

'I expect Annie will get in though,' said Sue.

'Ah, yes,' nodded Mara wisely. 'She never puts a foot wrong.'

Rebecca was relieved that they'd changed the

subject and even more relieved when – just as she was trying to stifle a yawn – Margot suddenly stood up, extended a hand and tugged her to her feet.

'Come on, you need a good night's sleep. Let's all go to our beds.'

'I'm glad we can lie in, in the morning,' murmured Rebecca, now in the middle of a really good yawn. 'I'm tired!'

She hung her party clothes up carefully, washed her face and cleaned her teeth. Then – in order not to talk to the other two – she got into bed and pulled the bedclothes right up over her head. Soon she was fast asleep.

'Give us an R!' shrilled a junior voice. It sounded like Lucy Hubbard's.

'R!' came the chorus.

'Give us an E –'

'E!'

'Give us a B –'

They spelt out Rebecca's name, letter by letter. With each letter the chorus got louder until finally –

'And what do you get?' chanted Lucy.

'REBECCA!'

'And who's going to win?'

'REBECCA!!'

The juniors had turned up in force at south courts to watch the match. The two players were warming up, knocking the ball back and forth, and the juniors were letting off steam whilst they could.

Rebecca didn't mind; she needed something to buoy her up!

She'd been a bag of nerves all morning, and glad to have half an hour on the phone with Robbie. He'd tried to tell her how to play her opponent. 'She's a defensive player – attack her, attack her! And run after everything – she lobs a lot – just keep getting everything back and she'll get demoralised because she won't have anything left. The other thing Rebecca – keep up the fast swerving service, you've really got it now . . .' And so on. That had all steadied her for a while.

But by two o'clock, Rebecca's legs were feeling like jelly again and she'd forbidden the others to come and watch her.

'If you come, I'll let you all down – I just *know* that's what will happen!'

'Oh, all right,' said Tish, disappointed. 'We'll push off to the beach then. Crikey, isn't it hot! Who'd ever have thought it?'

It had been a lonely moment, stepping out on to the court, though. The support from the juniors was just what she needed – it made her feel good but at the same time she knew they weren't nerveracked the way Tish & Co would have been.

'Give us an E!' shouted Nicola Hodges, whose money was on Eddie.

'E!' cried the pack.

'Give us a D –'

They were in full voice when Eddie walked up to Miss Darling in the umpire's chair.

'For goodness' sake, can't we tell these brats to shut up?' she asked.

So the prefect was on edge, too, Rebecca realised. That improved her spirits still further. But did Edwina have to look so bad-tempered? Didn't she *like* having supporters? 'Come on, let's make a game of it, then!' thought Rebecca.

Up in the chair, stiff-backed and unsmiling, Miss Darling produced a whistle and blew a long blast, at the same time lifting a hand for silence. She looked like a policeman on traffic duty.

'Let's begin!' she said.

Some distance away, beyond the old cedar tree, Pippa was putting the finishing touches to her painting. As she heard the whistle, she laid her brush down and got to her feet. Tall and elegant in a fully flared cotton skirt, she drifted across the school lawns in the direction of south courts. 'Might as well see how Rebecca gets on,' she thought.

Rebecca had never known such a hot sun in early May! It seemed to be right overhead, burning down on the top of her head. At times, as she raced backwards and forwards across the width of the court, up and down its length, retrieving each ball in turn, the build up of heat became so intense that she felt as though her arms and legs would melt away and the dry red dust of the court underfoot would fry her to a cinder.

Eddie Burton was a very deceptive player. Her service was quite slow. She played mainly from the baseline, sending down first a forehand, then a backhand, with such stolid unimaginativeness, that Rebecca at first became over-confident. There was no fire in Eddie's play – she would be easy to beat!

It wasn't until she suddenly found that she'd lost the first three games that Rebecca realised that her opponent was placing the ball with great skill. So often it looked as though it were going out and Rebecca would let it go, only to see it land right on the line, first in one corner of the court, then the other, and Eddie would get the vital point.

It was then that Robbie's words came back to her . . . run after everything . . . just keep getting everything back and she'll get demoralised because she won't have anything left.

Then began the marathon battle for supremacy between the two girls that kept Rebecca running, running, running, retrieving impossible-looking shots, inching her way back into the game until the score stood at 2–3 and the sweat was pouring down her face. Some of the rallies in those two games went to ten and fifteen strokes, and there were a dozen or more in each game.

Then, in the sixth game, came the most punishing rally of all. It was at game point for Rebecca. Backwards and forwards went the ball. Each time Rebecca got one of Eddie's stolidly walloped shots back, she would see it returned to the opposite side of the court and would have to race to retrieve it, white tennis shoes slithering through the red dust.

Finally on the twentieth stroke, Eddie relaxed – certain that she'd hit a winner: a cunning lob that sailed right over Rebecca's head and threw up a cloud of chalk on the baseline. Yet somehow Rebecca got there, tipped her racket to it in mid-sprint – sending it skimming back across the net out of Eddie's reach – before cannoning with some force into the wire netting at the back of the court.

Rebecca clung on to the wire netting, eyes closed, as she heard clapping and rapturous squeals from some of the juniors, somewhere behind her. She'd levelled 3–3! More than that. She was convinced, from the glimpse of despair she'd seen on Eddie's face just then, that her opponent would be the first to crack.

Gasping for breath, she opened her eyes and found herself staring straight into a familiar face. Pippa was right there, just on the other side of the wire netting.

'*Played*, Rebecca!' she whispered. 'For heaven's sake stop playing her game now and start playing your own.'

Rebecca was overjoyed. Pippa wanted her to win! She turned and ran and scooped up some balls to serve. In her mind she could hear Robbie at the end of the phone – *She's a defensive player – attack her, attack her!*

She threw a ball up, straight and high. Was it really only last summer that Pippa had first taught her how to do that? She turned her shoulders and racket head down into the ball . . .

Eddie just watched it spurt away through a cloud of chalk. An ace!

Rebecca had the killer instinct now. She won the game to love, then broke Eddie's service in the next game. She went on to hold her own service – with a series of lightning volleys up at the net – and the set was hers, 6–3.

'We'll leave it there,' Miss Darling said crisply. The girls had come up to the umpire's chair for a drink, preparing to change ends and start a second set. 'This sun is quite freakish. I think you've both done enough.'

The juniors came thronging round the gate.

'Shoo!' said Miss Darling. 'Off you go. Game's over.'

'Who's going in the team?' demanded Lucy Hubbard.

'Tell us.'

'Rebecca Mason. Now run away all of you. Go and have a swim.'

A swim! It was odd. That was all Rebecca could think about – getting cool.

'Congratulations,' said Edwina Burton, holding out a hand, stiffly.

'Thanks,' said Rebecca. It hadn't quite got through to her yet.

'You'll go in at third pair with Pippa Fellowes-Walker,' Miss Darling told Rebecca. 'Team practice six o'clock this evening. First cup match on Wednesday. Go off and enjoy the rest of the afternoon now.' For a moment it looked as though Miss Darling were going to smile! 'Well played, Rebecca.'

Rebecca walked off across the grass, in a daze. She looked round for Pippa, but there was no sign of her. As she drew close to the cedar tree she saw Pippa's easel beyond. She'd be back at any moment, surely. Rebecca wanted to tell her –

Suddenly she was out of the blistering sun and in deepest shade. Only then did Rebecca realise how hot she was – how hot and triumphantly exhausted!

She threw herself down under the cedar tree, turned on to her back, and placed her hands under her head . . . gazing up into the cool, green darkness above her. Oh, it was so beautiful! The sweeping branches gave such a dense shade, it made her feel as though she were already swimming in the sea.

'I'm in the team!' Rebecca told herself, out loud. It was only just beginning to dawn on her. 'I'm *in the team*!'

It was a moment of ecstasy.

She closed her eyes, opened them, closed them again. She was longing to see the others and tell them the news. Yet, somehow, she couldn't move a muscle. It was a reaction. Not to the physical effort, that wasn't so bad; but to the emotional strain of it all.

After the longest fortnight of her life, the suspense was over.

FOUR
A Perfect Term

The suspense was over! As Rebecca's mind uncoiled and luxuriated in the thought she opened her eyes again and stared up into the depths of the tree, letting the branches and the dark foliage swim in and out of focus. A little breeze came whispering down, brushing her cheeks. She could hear birds twittering and rustling up there somewhere.

Cool and green, dark and green, to lie below and feel serene . . .

Suddenly, inconsequentially, a poem started to form in her mind. She lay there, building it up, line by line. It was all about the old cedar tree and how generations of girls had lazed beneath it, on hot summer days . . . how they came and went . . . but the tree went on forever.

At last, she stirred.

'Don't move, Rebecca!' called a voice. 'Just two more minutes.'

Rebecca froze. That was Pippa's voice! Pippa was back at her easel, painting . . .

'Okay now. Come and see what you think.'

Rebecca got up slowly, picked up her tennis racket, and then walked out into the light, blinking. She went and joined Pippa, whose hair looked more golden than usual in the sun's rays. She found herself staring at the finished canvas.

The dark tree – the sunlight – the warm glow of school buildings beyond – everything was there.

And something had been added. A tiny figure in white reclining under the tree in an attitude of joy, ecstasy even, her racket lying in the grass beside her. Here the paint was new and glistening.

'It's me!' exclaimed Rebecca.

'Like it?' asked Pippa happily.

'*Yes*,' said Rebecca, overwhelmed to see herself in the picture.

'I just knew there was something missing!' nodded Pippa. She stood up and took a few paces back, well pleased. 'It needed a figure in it . . . a mood . . . something elusive . . . and then you gave me the answer, Rebecca. Just like that!'

'It – it's a beautiful painting,' said Rebecca, quite overawed. 'It'll make a most stunning cover for the magazine this term.'

'It sums it up for me now,' said Pippa. 'I don't think it's great art or anything, but I hope it'll mean something to other people too. Those who've left, I mean, who get the magazine. I think – I hope – it sums up what a happy place Trebizon is. Somehow this . . .'

Her voice began to trail away.

'. . . the cedar tree . . . the sunshine . . . the tennis term . . . this is how I'll always remember Trebizon.

When I've gone.'

There was a long silence.

'And you got in the team?' Pippa said at last. 'As if I need ask!'

Rebecca smiled.

'I missed the last bit. Annie wanted me. But I could see you were in! We'll have to get used to playing together, Rebecca. That will be interesting.' She smiled at her. 'You'll be the baby of the team, won't you!'

'There's a team practice after tea!' Rebecca said.

Then she continued to stare at the picture.

'I made up a poem just then,' she volunteered. 'About the tree.'

'Write it then!' said Pippa, lightly. 'You never know . . . let's see, I haven't had Third Year's in, have I?'

'Helena keeps reminding us but she hasn't given us a deadline yet,' said Rebecca. 'Not as far as I know!'

'She'd better get a move on!' observed Pippa. 'We go to press soon.'

That galvanised Rebecca. She'd forgo the swim! She'd make do with a shower.

'I think I'll go and write it now – before I forget it!'

She sprinted off across the grass, making for the track by the rhododendrons that led through to Court House. Pippa smiled again and packed up her easel and stool, every so often glancing at her finished canvas.

It was good to have it done and know that it was right at last.!

This term, surely, was going to turn out to be everything she hoped for – a perfect term!

It was going to be a perfect term! Those were exactly Rebecca's sentiments, too, when she went to bed that Sunday evening, exhausted and happy.

She'd scrawled out her poem in rough and finished it just as Tish and the others came rushing into Court House, dripping wet and still in swimsuits, to find her. They'd heard the news from some juniors on the beach.

'Rebeck!'

'What are you doing hiding up here?'

'Whoopieeee!'

'Let's phone Robbie –'

'Let's have a party tonight!'

After that it had been non-stop activity. Phone calls to Syon, the boys' boarding house at Garth

College. They'd meet them at Fenners for a celebration later on . . . Curly and Chris and Mike and Sue's brothers David and Edward – and maybe Robbie as well.

Their high spirits overflowed into the big school dining hall at tea time so that three times the duty mistress, Miss Heath, had to tell them all to be quiet. Then they rushed over to south courts to watch Rebecca take part in team practice – even though it only turned out to be some coaching with Miss Darling.

Then – great excitement – Pippa let them all see her painting, over at Parkinson House. It was laid out on a big table ready for a meeting of *The Journal* editorial committee that night. Rebecca had told them all about it.

The evening consisted of cycling down town to Fenners to meet the boys and laughing and talking and drinking coffee and eating cream cakes – then the whole gang of them came cycling back to Court House to ask Mrs Barrington if they could play some records in the Common Room. A noisy party in the house across the street from Fenners had put them in the mood.

'Certainly not! It's about time you girls got some

sleep. You've been rushing around like giddy goats.'

She shook a finger at the boys, as they crowded round the porch.

'Shooo!'

Margaret Exton looked down over the banisters as Rebecca and her friends tumbled into the main hall, yelling and laughing and shoving one another.

'You'd think nobody ever got into a team before,' she said to Alison Hissup, who'd taken her own selection very calmly.

'They're in the most stupid mood I've ever seen them in, and that's saying something.'

'Well, as long as they don't try and climb the clock tower or something,' yawned Alison. 'Is that the phone ringing?'

It was for Rebecca.

'Robbie!' she squealed.

'Oh, spare us!' sniffed Margaret, turning to continue her way upstairs.

But that call made Rebecca's day complete.

'Sorry I couldn't get to Fenners,' said Robbie. He was working hard now for his GCSEs. 'Clever girl.I'd have given you a big kiss!'

'Thanks for all you did to help me, Robbie,' said Rebecca.

'*Rebecca!*' said Mrs Barrington sternly, looking into the hall.

'Goodnight, Robbie,' she said hastily. 'Got to go now!'

Yes, it was going to be a perfect term!

But at midnight that night, the trouble started.

FIVE
Roll Call in the Middle of the Night

'Whassat?' asked Sue sleepily. It seemed like the middle of the night and she could hear someone moving around in the room.

'It's only me,' whispered Rebecca. 'Just going to get a drink of water.'

She felt her way out, past the beds, opened the door and crept into the narrow corridor on the ground floor, where all the Third Year rooms in Court House were located. There was a dim light burning and she tiptoed along to the kitchen. What was the time? It must be at least midnight by now.

The trouble was she couldn't get to sleep. Too much excitement!

They'd carried on whispering and laughing and

running in and out of each other's rooms after lights out. When Rebecca had finally tumbled into bed she'd found it felt really peculiar. She'd tossed and turned and tried to get some sleep – only to discover that Tish and Aba had collected up some tennis rackets and put them in layers between her blankets!

That had created more hilarity and it had taken the appearance of Mrs Barrington to put a stop to it all.

'If there's one more sound from this corridor, you'll all have a detention tomorrow!' she'd said wearily.

They'd all gone to sleep after that – except Rebecca. She was too elated!

She kept dozing and then waking up again, with a start, remembering that she was in the tennis team! She would re-live the match she'd played against Eddie Burton, especially that long rally, stroke by stroke . . . and remember the way Pippa had painted her into the picture, afterwards.

The lines of the poem kept going through her mind, too, and she wondered if she'd get it accepted for the magazine. Then she started thinking about their first cup match, on Wednesday. It was against

Caxton High. They weren't bad! They played tennis all the year round there . . .

She must get to sleep! Perhaps a drink of water would help.

In the kitchen, she turned on the light and looked for a cup.

Eerily, in the silence of the night, she heard the distant sound of a telephone ringing in the other part of the house where the Barringtons lived. Then it stopped.

She turned on the tap, rinsed the cup out, then filled it to the brim and drank it down. Her throat had been quite dry. It must have been all the laughing and running about, much earlier. Feeling better, she washed and dried the cup, put it away and came out of the kitchen, switching the light off behind her. As she stepped back into the gloom of the corridor a shocked voice came from the darkness.

'Rebecca!'

It was Mrs Barrington, in her dressing gown, hurrying through the private door from her own wing of the house. Her face was white!

She came straight up to Rebecca and put an arm round her shoulders.

'You silly, silly girl!' she exclaimed, keeping her

voice low. 'What's all this about running away? Miss Welbeck's coming right over. Whatever's the matter?'

'Running away?' gasped Rebecca. Her mouth fell open. *Running away!*

'Wasn't that you, then?'

'What, Mrs Barry? Me, what?'

The House Mistress was staring at the phone in the main hall, just a few feet away. She pointed to it.

'Who phoned Miss Welbeck then? Someone's just rung her from here. She's getting her car and coming over right away – she'll be here in a minute.'

'What on earth did they say?' exclaimed Rebecca.

'Just –' Mrs Barrington frowned, adjusting her mind to the idea that it hadn't been Rebecca. 'Just that they hated Court House and would be gone by the morning! It – it wasn't you, then?'

'No!'

'But you're up! You must have seen somebody? Maybe it was you who disturbed them – they rang off in a hurry, it seems.'

Rebecca started to shake her head, baffled, when they heard the sound of a car outside and the glass panel of the front door was briefly illuminated by brilliant headlights. 'The Principal!' exclaimed Mrs Barrington.

She put the main lights on in the hall and hurried to let her in.

Miss Welbeck strode in, wearing an old fur coat and a headscarf, bringing some of the cool night air in with her. She looked tense.

'Rebecca –?' she began.

'It wasn't Rebecca and she didn't see anybody,' said the House Mistress quickly.

'Then the girl's already gone!' rapped Miss Welbeck.

She glanced up the staircase.

'Get everybody out of bed, Joan,' she said, decisively. 'There's nothing else for it. You'd better get everyone up and take a roll call. If a girl's run away the first thing we have to know is who it is.'

Rebecca just blinked. Every moment that passed, this began to seem more and more like a dream.

It was chaotic!

Mrs Barrington sounded the rising bell in the middle of the night.

Girls started to emerge pyjama-ed and dressing-gowned in all stages of sleep, blinking and yawning and protesting as lights went on and they were herded out of their rooms, along corridors and down stairs, until they were all together in one large herd in the big Common Room.

'Right, this won't take long,' said Miss Welbeck crisply. She nodded at Mrs Barrington, who had the full house list in her hand.

'Aba Amori –'

'Present!'

'Ishbel Anderson –'

'Present!' said Tish, trying not to giggle with nerves.

'Jane Bowen –'

'Present!'

The House Mistress ticked the names off one by one.

'Amanda Hancock –'

'Present!'

'Alison Hissup –'

'Present!'

'Elizabeth Kendall –'

On she went, working her way down the list. It was unreal, like a fantasy, thought Rebecca. Some tendrils of ivy tapped against the big bay windows of the Common Room and an owl hooted somewhere in the blackness.

A roll call in the middle of the night!

'Virginia Slade –'

'Present!'

'And Sarah Turner –'

'Present!'

So that was that. Thirty-six girls – all present and correct!

Mrs Barrington and the Principal exchanged looks.

'Thank you, girls,' said Miss Welbeck. 'You may all return to your beds when I say. But somebody spoke to me on the phone a few minutes ago and said she was running away. I must know who it was. Would the girl step forward, please?'

Nobody moved.

'Very well,' said Miss Welbeck, after a minute's silence. 'Go back to bed all of you. No talking.'

They all crushed out of the Common Room, the most senior girls first, anxious to get back to their warm beds but already starting to whisper and exclaim over the sensational happening, as soon as they were out of earshot of the Common Room.

'Wait a moment, Rebecca.'

Miss Welbeck questioned her closely. Why was she up after midnight? Was she sure she'd seen nobody in the hall? What had woken her up – might it have been the sound of a girl using the phone?

Rebecca just shook her head. She'd been awake for some time. No one used the phone. She would have heard them. She just got up to get a drink of water, that was all.

Miss Welbeck sent her back to bed.

'Now what do we do?' asked Mrs Barrington, softly closing the door. 'It looks as though the girl only *said* she was ringing from Court House. Could you not hear her voice well enough to recognise who it was?'

'No,' said Miss Welbeck, thoughtfully. 'It was rather muffled – *gasping* – as though she were trying not to cry.'

'Should we alert the other boarding houses?' asked Mrs Barrington, in some alarm. 'Perhaps the whole school had better be checked. What should we do?' she repeated.

'Nothing,' said Miss Welbeck, shortly.

'Nothing?'

The Principal wrapped her coat closer round her. She was preparing to go. She looked extremely annoyed.

'I thought the girl was trying not to cry. On reflection, I think she must have been trying not to laugh. I may live to regret it, but I don't intend to rouse the whole school at this time of night.'

'Then –'

'I seem to be the victim of a hoax,' said Miss Welbeck. 'And I am not amused.'

She walked over to the door and started to turn the handle.

'Would you do one last thing before you go back to bed, Joan?'

'Of course.'

'I saw no sign of a glass of water in Rebecca

Mason's hand. Check round the kitchen – see if there's any sign of a glass having been used.'

'Very well. But I'm sure Rebecca was speaking the truth.'

'One hopes so. It would be nice to have her story confirmed, though.'

Miss Welbeck was right. It was a hoax.

Monday morning dawned sunny and the school population was quite intact. No girl had run away from Court House, or any other boarding house.

'I ask the practical joker to report to my study immediately after Assembly,' the Principal told the packed hall. 'If she doesn't, it will be very much the worse for her.'

But nobody responded to Miss Welbeck's invitation.

The whole school was astonished by the hoax and everybody talked about it. Some might have considered it a mildly funny happening if it hadn't involved Miss Welbeck. But she was greatly admired and respected. The juniors were quite upset to see her angry and tight-lipped. It cast a cloud over the day.

The question on everybody's lips was – who would

have had the nerve? And what was there to gain from it? It was all, apparently, thoroughly pointless.

'Somebody with a twisted sense of humour in your house then, Maggie,' commented one of the girls in IV Alpha at morning break.

'Oh, yes, we've got our share of lunatics,' replied Margaret Exton.

'Poor Miss Welbeck,' said somebody else.

'What about poor us?' asked Margaret, eyes glittering a bit. 'It was quite frightening, being dragged out of bed in the middle of the night, all because of some stupid idiot.' She was squeezing the last drop of drama out of the situation. 'I'd like to get my hands on them!'

'Virginia Slade was in tears at breakfast and said she hadn't been able to get back to sleep all night.'

'Oh, she never can,' said Suky Morris, who was just passing. 'Every time she has a row with Mark Enwright the whole of V Beta has to hear about it – how she couldn't get a wink of sleep –'

'She said she was going to die of a broken heart last Saturday!'

'Whoever did it,' resumed Margaret Exton, not welcoming the change of subject, 'is for the high jump. That's for sure.'

'Got any ideas?'

'It could have been one of Tish Anderson's crowd,' said Margaret. 'They were in a pretty daft mood last night. And d'you know what –' she lowered her voice '– Rebecca Mason had to stay behind after Mrs Barry had checked the roll. Miss Welbeck wanted to know what she was doing *up*.'

By tea time a whole host of rumours was flying around Trebizon.

It was Rebecca Mason, she'd been seen near the phone at midnight.

No, it was Tish Anderson and Rebecca Mason had covered up for her.

No again – it was definitely Rebecca Mason – Mrs Barry had caught her with the phone in her hand.

No – it was neither of those – it was Virginia Slade. Mark Enwright had dropped her – it was a cry for help.

But by Monday evening, after much heart searching, Miss Welbeck had formed a theory of her own.

'A motive, Evelyn,' she confided in the senior maths mistress. 'One has to look for a motive! I think it might have been a member of Parkinson House –'

'But Madeleine, how could it –' began Miss Gates.

'I'll give her a day or two to come to her senses. If nobody's come forward by Wednesday, I shall invite her to my study and ask some very searching questions.'

Miss Welbeck sighed. It was all very tiresome.

'I can't be sure, of course,' she admitted.

SIX
The Missing Number

'Some people think it was you, Rebecca!' Tish said indignantly, at breakfast on Tuesday morning. 'Or me!'

This term she'd taken over Joss Vining's place as head of their table in dining hall. She was at present dishing out pieces of bacon from an oval serving dish.

Keeping her ear to the ground as only Tish could, she'd picked up some displeasing vibrations.

'Who cares –' said Rebecca, pronging her bacon, '– what some people think? Miss Welbeck'll track the person down sooner or later.'

She was fed up with thinking about the hoax. There were other, more important things to think about.

She'd missed the final notice asking for magazine contributions to be given in. She'd got her poem in to Helena King, over at Norris House, only just in the nick of time!

As this year's Magazine Officer, Helena's job was to shortlist all Third Year contributions for *The Trebizon Journal* and then organise a vote to be taken for the best. They would then go forward to Pippa and her committee and inclusion in *The Journal* was more or less guaranteed. It was all very democratic.

She'd got the poem in yesterday.

The magazine meeting, with the vote, was today!

There was also the question of a maths test, first lesson. Miss Hort wasn't too pleased with the way Rebecca's trigonometry was going and Rebecca badly wanted to sort out the difference between sines and cosines once and for all, before the test. Preferably with Tish, if only she'd stop going on about the hoax.

Most important of all, there was a two-hour team practice this afternoon to get the new pairs used to playing together. Rebecca had been told that Jilly and Alison, the second pair, were to play at least three sets against her and Pippa, the third pair. Della and Kate, who'd played together for years, would just play singles.

Tomorrow they were playing Caxton High School in the first round of the inter-schools cup! It was a knockout tournament so if Trebizon were beaten tomorrow, they were out of the cup. Thank goodness they were playing at home, thought Rebecca, so there'd be a good crowd to cheer them on. She wondered anxiously what it was going to be like playing as Pippa's partner and whether Pippa would still be pleased that she'd got into the team instead of Eddie Burton!

'What are you daydreaming about?' asked Mara with a smile.

'Er –' Rebecca looked guilty. 'Nothing really. Trigonometry, I suppose.'

'At *breakfast*?' exclaimed Sue.

In fact, with Tish's help, Rebecca sorted out her maths problem before lessons started and managed to get seven out of ten in the test, which got her day off to a good start.

In the lunch hour they trooped up to the form room for the Third Year magazine meeting. Margot and Elf had helpfully drummed up the support of all ground floor residents in Court House (with the exception of Aba, who was having some athletics coaching with Angela Hessel) to come along and vote for Rebecca's poem.

But to Rebecca's relief there wasn't even a contest.

'I've only been given two items this term,' said Helena, 'and both of them are terrific. If you all agree, we'll hand them both in together and they can be our contributions for this issue.'

She then read out Rebecca's poem and passed round a beautiful pen-and-ink drawing that Verity Williams had done of her pony, Brandy, in the Easter holidays. Everybody was very impressed and the vote in favour of both items going in was unanimous.

'I'll take them straight over to Parkinson now,' said Helena, putting them back in her folder, 'and give them to Pippa.'

When she reached the Upper Sixth boarding house, Pippa and Annie were sitting in Pippa's car. Annie wound down the window and reached out a hand.

'Thanks, I'll take them.'

Pippa had both hands on the steering wheel and was gazing ahead, preoccupied. Annie put the folder on the back seat, then smoothed down her fair hair. A few moments later, they drove off.

Meanwhile, Rebecca and Verity were so delighted at the way things had gone, they took everybody to Moffatt's and bought barley sugars all round.

Rebecca half hoped that Pippa might say something about the poem at the tennis practice that afternoon. But she didn't.

They took a while to settle down together. Pippa's concentration seemed poor and Rebecca was nervous. She'd hang back to let Pippa take shots that were strictly speaking hers, which Pippa promptly missed.

'Sorry!' she kept saying.

'Rebecca Mason, wake up!' barked Miss Darling. 'Just because you're the baby of the team that doesn't mean you have to behave like one! And stop saying "sorry"!'

Rebecca then overreacted and went to the other extreme – plunging in to take every ball so that twice she and Pippa clashed rackets and she would find herself saying 'sorry' again. But Pippa was patient and good-humoured. The problem was they were cast in the same mould, fluent and graceful players who were good all round the court. But slowly they worked out a pattern for playing together.

At the opposite end of the court Alison and Jilly had settled down together much more quickly. Jilly, with her towering height, was brilliant at the net whereas Alison was strong and sound playing back from the baseline. They took the first set easily, 6–1.

However, by the second set Pippa and Rebecca were beginning to build up their own strategy for covering the court and – although they lost again – there were some exciting rallies. The third and final set was long and hard-fought. When they finally ran out the losers at 7–9, Rebecca was exhausted but happy.

'I feel we've been playing together for years now, don't you?' smiled Pippa, as she zipped her racket into its waterproof cover. 'I'm quite looking forward to the match tomorrow!'

'So am I!' said Rebecca, though not without a churning sensation in the pit of her stomach. 'They're good, aren't they?'

'Not as good as us!' said Pippa.

Miss Darling gathered the whole team around and gave them a pep talk. She also told them all to have an early night.

'Especially you, Rebecca.'

Rebecca did her prep straight after tea – French and history – then amazed her friends by going off to have a bath and wash her hair at seven o'clock. After that, while her hair dried, she sewed her First VI colours on to her white tennis dress, rinsed it through by hand and then went along to the laundry room and dried it in the tumble dryer.

She'd just fished it out when Tish burst in, dishevelled, in her tracksuit, having just been for a practice run along the beach – she was running in the 800 metres on Sports Day.

'How do I look?' asked Rebecca, laughing with excitement and holding her sparklingly clean dress up against her dressing gown. 'D'you like the team colours? Oh, Tish, I still can't believe I've got them!'

Tish jerked her thumb. 'You're wanted on the phone.'

It was Pippa.

'Rebecca – I read your poem at tea time. And we've just had an editorial meeting. We all love it! We're going to superimpose it on the picture of the cedar tree, just at the bottom where the grass is. I thought you'd like to know.'

'On – on the cover?' gasped Rebecca.

'That's right. Going to bed early?'

'Yes.' Rebecca felt a sense of mounting excitement. 'Oh, Pippa, my parents will be so thrilled. I'll order some copies for them.'

Mr and Mrs Mason were in Saudi Arabia and could never get to Trebizon. They'd only seen the school once, but their thoughts were always with Rebecca, whom they missed.

'It's pretty hot and dusty where they are, isn't it?' said Pippa. 'Hope they like our nice cool cedar tree to look at! Night, Rebecca.'

Rebecca put the phone down and stood there a while, dazed, staring at the wall in front of her. There was a list of school phone numbers pinned up there, giving the numbers of all the other boarding houses. Rebecca gazed at them, blankly, thinking about her phone call.

'Sue! Tish! Mara!' she cried, at last. 'Guess what –!'

She rushed into the kitchen and told them.

'What a term you're having!' exclaimed Sue. 'Wow-ee!'

Rebecca went to bed early and was nearly asleep when the others came in. She'd been thinking about tomorrow's match, feeling keyed up and excited. But suddenly, for no reason, the list of numbers by the coinbox came back to her mind. She could see them very clearly.

'Hey. That's funny,' she said, opening her eyes.

'What's funny?' asked Sue.

'The list of numbers by the phone. Miss Welbeck's home number isn't up there –'

'Of course it isn't,' said Sue. 'It's private. I suppose the staff have got it.' She giggled. 'Want to give her a ring?'

'I was thinking about the hoaxer,' said Rebecca.

'Hey, yes!' said Tish. She was doing a headstand on the bed, but quickly turned herself the right way up. 'That's interesting. How many girls know Miss

Welbeck's number? I don't.'

'Nor me,' said Sue.

'None of us do,' yawned Rebecca.

Tish bounced up and down on the bed a few times, using it as a trampoline. Finally she got in between the covers and picked up a book.

'When I get the chance I'm going to tell Miss Welbeck that!'

Rebecca turned over. It was the match tomorrow – she didn't want to think about the hoaxer any more.

But, as things turned out, she was going to have to.

SEVEN
Fire!

Wednesday dawned cool and dull. The early May weather was back to normal.

'Good!' said Sue, jumping out of bed and drawing back the curtains. 'That means there'll be some spectators this afternoon.'

Rebecca laughed.

Wednesday was a half-day for the Middle and Upper School and if it were sunny this afternoon, counter-attractions like swimming and surfing would draw most girls away from watching the cup match. But it wasn't going to be sunny!

It looked as though there'd be a good crowd along.

At the end of morning lessons, a lot of III Alpha wished Rebecca luck. Afterwards, in the dining hall, girls from III Beta and Gamma came up as well. Joss may have gone but now they had someone else from the Third Year in the team.

'Hope you win, Rebecca!' said Roberta Jones, who was on the next table. 'Hear you've got something in the magazine as well.'

Roberta was much more settled these days, now that she had three close friends in Norris House – Debbie Rickard and the Nathan twins.

'The way she used to fight and struggle to get something in the magazine herself!' commented Sue, afterwards. 'When we were juniors. And she couldn't write for toffee!'

'It was *embarrassing*,' said Mara.

'Max changed her,' said Rebecca, remembering. 'That was one good thing he did. Do you realise that was only a year ago? It seems much longer, somehow.'

'Lot's happened since then!' said Margot. She smiled, showing her beautiful white teeth. 'I bet you never dreamt then what you'd be doing today. Oh, Rebecca – we're all dying to see you play!'

'Supposing we're knocked out in the first round? I ought to be scared but I'm not really,' said Rebecca. She thought about it. 'I'm looking forward to it. To playing with Pippa!'

Lady Edwina came by at that moment.

'You'd better make a good job of it this afternoon,' she said, with a half-smile. 'Good luck.'

'I'll try,' said Rebecca. It was the first time the older girl had spoken to her directly since the trials and the half-smile was all she could manage. 'Thanks, Eddie.'

In the lunch hour the six friends went down to Trebizon Bay, through the little wicket gate at the back of Juniper House and up over the sand dunes. The skies were grey and the big flat expanse of sand was almost deserted. The sea was fairly rough, tossing great breakers to the shore and the gulls were wheeling and crying round the empty beach huts.

'Not beach weather,' said Elf. 'I'm glad really.'

'It's only just tennis weather,' said Margot, looking up at the skies. 'I wonder if it's going to rain?'

'I don't think so,' said Sue.

'I like it!' exclaimed Rebecca, climbing back up one of the sand dunes, flinging her arms wide and taking some deep breaths at the top. 'It's nice when it's hot, but it's lovely when it's like this and you've got the whole bay to yourself.'

She breathed in the tangy sea air and watched a tanker move very slowly across the horizon. She was amazed how relaxed she felt, with the big match just over an hour away. It had been a good idea to have an early night!

At two o'clock they split up.

The match wasn't until three. Before settling down to watch it, Sue, Mara, Margot and Elf wanted to do something energetic. They decided to go over to the sports centre and play badminton and maybe have a swim in the indoor pool. But Tish had already been on a long run, before breakfast, and now she had some things she needed to look up for her history project. That meant going over to the library.

'What will you do, Rebeck?'

'Just wander back to Court House and get ready. Then go over to meet Caxton.'

The minibus from Caxton High was due at main school at two-thirty and the First VI were to meet it. They'd been told to welcome their opponents and make them feel at home before the match.

After she'd changed into her tennis dress and put her tracksuit on, Rebecca began to feel restless. She put a ball in her pocket, picked up her racket and wandered along the path past the Hilary and the little lake until old building came in sight. She went across to the main entrance, but there was no one around. Squinting at the clock tower she saw that it was still only quarter past two.

Fifteen minutes until the Caxton lot arrived! And there was no sign of Kate or Pippa or any of the others. Rebecca skirted round the old manor house to a quiet place she knew and started knocking a tennis ball against the side wall there. No harm in loosening up a bit!

Meanwhile Tish, who tended to do everything in a rush, had already found what she needed in the library and scribbled some dates down.

The library was on the ground floor of the former manor house and was one of its finest rooms, its windows facing to the front. It was always a very peaceful place, but today it was unusually peaceful for the simple reason that two prefects had just gone out and it was now completely empty.

Tish was a gregarious person and besides, Rebecca was very much in her thoughts.

'May as well hang around in the main hall for five minutes and spy for the bus to arrive,' she thought.

She opened the library door and peered out along

the wide corridor which in the distance opened out on to the main hall. But she immediately withdrew and closed the door again. There was a senior in a tracksuit just inside the main entrance, leaning against the wall.

Tish roamed around, looking at the books, then cautiously opened the door again. But she was still there whoever she was – leaning against the wall and staring up the main staircase, as though waiting for somebody! So Tish withdrew into the library again and this time went and knelt on one of the window seats, peering out.

She craned her neck.

'I can see from here!' she realised.

There was no sign of Rebecca, but two or three other members of the team were wandering across the gravelled forecourt, carrying tennis rackets, ready to meet the bus when it came. Tish watched them for a while.

It must be nearly half-past two . . .

Brrrrrnnng! Brrrrrrrrnnnnnnn . . .

Tish nearly jumped out of her skin as a bell rang loudly and continuously outside the library. It went on and on and on . . .

What on earth?

'Fire practice!' she thought. Then – 'No, it can't be!'

They wouldn't have fire practice on a half-day, when most of the classrooms were empty! And visitors from another school due to arrive any minute!

She rushed out of the library. She could hear bells ringing all over the building! She went clammy all over. *It was a real fire! It must be!*

She raced along to the big entrance hall, her foot tinkling through some broken glass at the foot of the main stairs – looking round fearfully for sign of smoke or flames. Then she saw the coinbox phone on the wall beyond the stairs and rushed over to it.

Fire! What did you do? You pressed –

9 . . . 9 . . . 9.

'Which service do you require?' asked a cool voice.

'Fire!' gulped Tish. 'Trebizon School! The old building's on fire. Tell them to come quickly!'

She put the phone down. What next? Of course, fire drill.

They'd practised it often enough. File out of the building in an orderly manner, make for the main forecourt in front of old building. Line up in forms in strict alphabetical order . . .

As she pushed open the main doors to go outside, she heard a babble on the main staircase behind her – many voices talking at once and, rising above, the calm tones of Miss Welbeck.

'All out girls. No need to panic –'

More girls were gathering in the forecourt outside. Rebecca was coming this way, with her tennis racket.

'Tish!'

She hurried up.

'What's happening? Is it a real fire? I was round the side and suddenly I heard all these bells ringing inside the building –'

'They're still ringing!' said Tish, jerking her head towards the building. 'It must be a real fire! I rang 999!'

Inside, Miss Welbeck and Mrs Devenshire the school secretary were now standing at the foot of the main staircase, shepherding dozens of scurrying juniors out of the building. They'd been having lessons up in the top classrooms. Some of them were making their way down fire escapes at the back of the building. Everything was under control.

'Don't run!' rapped Miss Welbeck. She tapped aside some fragments of broken glass with her toe and looked all round for any signs of smoke. 'This may well be a false alarm. Just go to the far side of the forecourt in an orderly manner –'

Outside, Rebecca linked her arm through Tish's.

'We'd better go and line up,' she said.

Girls were coming from all directions now, dozens and dozens of them. Not just from the old building, but from Juniper House round at the back and from various parts of the grounds. Well drilled, they were all converging on the main forecourt.

Rebecca and Tish went and stood far back from the building now, over by the trees. They stared up at all the windows in turn.

'I wonder where the fire is?' said Rebecca in awe. 'Can't see anything.'

'Perhaps it's round the back,' said Alison Hissup.

'The alarm bells have stopped ringing,' said Tish.

At that moment Miss Jameson, the senior games mistress at Caxton High School, was just turning the school's brand new minibus into the Trebizon grounds. She drove carefully along the narrow track, observing the ten mph speed limit when suddenly she heard a tremendous din behind her.

Screaming siren – flashing lights – there was something big and red right on her tail!

'A *fire engine!*' shrieked her passengers. 'There's a fire!'

Something close to panic seized Miss Jameson, as she looked in her driving mirror. She was driving a minibus-load of excitable girls along a difficult track at its most narrow point, with overhanging trees and bushes on either side, and this huge noisy thing behind, wailing like a banshee, seemed to be wanting to run her down.

At first she tried to accelerate and get ahead of it, only to find the minibus swerving alarmingly on the bumpy track.

'You can get off – look over there!' cried someone.

She saw what looked like a flat smooth clearing to the right, pulled over hard and got off the school drive to let the fire engine past – only to find that she was skidding into mud! As the fire engine roared on its way, the minibus slowly bumped to a halt against a tree, denting the front nearside wing.

'Streuth!' said Miss Jameson.

The girls had to get out to push the vehicle out of the mud.

Then, carefully, Miss Jameson reversed back on to the drive, took the girls back on board then slowly continued her journey along the school drive, with the front wing making a nasty little sound as it scraped against the wheel.

'This is a fine start,' she said.

When they arrived at the school, they found the forecourt lined with scores of girls and firemen swarming in and out of the building. Nobody even noticed them arrive.

But within a matter of minutes, everything fizzled out.

The firemen had all emerged from the building. Their chief spoke to the Principal, then they all got on to their fire engine and drove away again. The crowds of girls began to disperse. Crocodiles of junior girls were led back into the building to finish their first lesson.

There was no fire.

'You should have checked, ma'am, before calling us in,' the fire chief had told the Trebizon Principal.

It was, it seemed, a hoax. Apparently some idiot had smashed one of the glass fire alarm panels in the main building and then called 999.

'Fine bunch of clowns we've got here,' said the captain of Caxton tennis team.

Miss Darling came up then. Trailing behind her came the Trebizon team and one or two other girls, including Tish.

'I'm terribly sorry about all this –' she began.

'Look at our new minibus!' said Miss Jameson. 'We'll have to claim on insurance! It was the fire engine. The fire service should pay –'

They all gathered round.

'Oh,' said Pippa, upset.

Rebecca and Tish looked at each other. Tish felt guilty.

'I'd better go and own up,' she whispered.

'Own up?' asked Pippa sharply.

But Miss Welbeck, who had seen Tish using the phone earlier, was already bearing down on them.

She was feeling angry. Angry because she'd jumped to the wrong conclusion on Monday – about the identity of the hoaxer. She'd nearly made a fool of herself over that. And even angrier that a second hoax had been played, this time one that involved the whole school and the local fire service as well.

The hoaxer must be found!

'I'm sorry that your match has been slightly delayed,' she said to Miss Jameson, smiling courteously, her anger hidden. 'I hear it promises to be an exciting one, by all accounts.'

She signalled to Miss Darling and the Trebizon team to take the visitors off. Miss Darling responded quickly.

'Would you like to come and get changed?'

Miss Jameson cast an anxious glance towards the bumper.

'Hodkin will see to that, during the course of the afternoon,' said Miss Welbeck. 'I'm sure he can straighten it out enough to see you home safely.'

As they all moved away, Miss Welbeck turned to Tish.

'Would you come to my study please, Ishbel?' she asked in a pleasant voice. 'I believe you phoned the fire brigade?'

'Yes, Miss Welbeck,' said Tish, feeling slightly sick.

Pippa and Rebecca both glanced back and saw Tish being led away. So did Alison Hissup.

'Looks like we've found the hoaxer then,' she said. 'Tish Anderson. Well – honestly!'

EIGHT
... And Tish Gets a Grilling

Miss Darling ground her teeth. It was really too much!

They were over at the sports centre now, waiting in the foyer while the girls from Caxton High School got ready for the match.

Miss Darling was trying to engage Miss Jameson in polite conversation. As if that weren't difficult enough, with the visiting teacher in a bad mood because of the minibus, Trebizon's tennis coach could distinctly hear Rebecca and Alison squabbling!

'Take that back!'

'Why should I?'

She knew they'd been bickering for some time. At first they'd kept their voices low, but now they were starting to raise them. 'Pippa – come here a minute!' rasped Miss Darling as the prefect passed close to her.

'Yes, Miss Darling?'

'Tell those two to *shut up*,' she said, out of the corner of her mouth. Then, in the same breath, turning back to Miss Jameson. 'Yes, I do agree with you about grass courts.'

Pippa went over to Rebecca and Alison. They were both looking flushed and angry. Alison was in full flow –

'Well *somebody* phoned Miss Welbeck up from Court House on Sunday night and if it wasn't your lot who was it? You were stupid enough for anything – the racket you were making.'

'It wasn't us –'

'I suppose you thought it was funny. Now you've been at it again. What a time to choose! We'll never live it down – the Caxton lot'll be talking about it for years.'

Rebecca was almost in tears, all the more so because Alison Hissup was usually a friendly, easy-going person and the last person she'd expect to quarrel with. She turned to Pippa, helplessly.

'Alison just won't listen!' she said in despair.

'I don't blame her,' said Kate Hissup, joining the

group. 'These hoaxes are just a bit too much!' She looked at Rebecca suspiciously. But then she put a hand on her younger sister's shoulder. 'Cool it, Ally.'

'Look here!' said Pippa, finding her voice at last. She put an arm round Rebecca's shoulders, protectively. 'What is this – the Day of Judgement or something? I don't think Rebecca's crowd had anything to do with the hoaxes at *all*. Phoning the fire brigade doesn't mean anything.'

'Come off it –' Alison began to laugh.

To Rebecca's amazement Pippa went quite pale. She stamped her foot.

'Stop it, Alison!' she cried, flaring up. 'You can't go around accusing people of things when you haven't a shred of proof. You're making me sick, the whole lot of you. I think you should *apologise*.'

There was a stunned silence. Pippa, the gentlest and most sweet-tempered of people, was really angry!

Alison stared at the ground, uncomfortably.

'Sorry, Rebecca,' she mumbled.

' 's okay,' said Rebecca, catching in her breath as she looked at Pippa.

Even Kate was shamefaced. 'Pippa's dead right,' she said. At that moment the rival team emerged, all ready for the match. 'Time to start!' cried Kate, in relief. 'Come on, let's forget all this and get on with it.'

They ran out on to the school's new hard courts, just behind the sports centre, and a cheer went up.

'Come on, Trebizon!' cried Mara, Elf, Margot and Sue, together.

'Give us a T!' shouted someone.

'T!'

'Give us an R –'

'R!'

Rebecca hoped she was going to be able to concentrate. What was happening to Tish? she wondered. The quarrel with Alison had somehow thrown her off balance. Pippa looked upset, too. In fact, she looked so upset that Rebecca felt guilty. She shouldn't have dragged Pippa into it!

It seemed that although there were emergency fire buttons all over the school, only one had been triggered off. That was the one in the main entrance hall, near the door. Someone had deliberately smashed the glass panel, to release the emergency button. It had happened only seconds before Tish rushed out of the library.

Now, in the Principal's study, Tish was being cross-examined.

'You didn't see anybody running away?' repeated Miss Welbeck. 'Surely you caught a glimpse of somebody – heard footsteps running, perhaps? They do echo, you know.'

'Nobody,' repeated Tish. 'The place was empty.'

'You must have noticed something,' insisted Miss Welbeck.

'Nothing,' said Tish stubbornly.

'I see,' sighed Miss Welbeck. She pursed her lips, watching Tish. Then she spoke again. 'Let's go back to this girl in a tracksuit you happened to notice standing in the entrance hall, earlier. You glimpsed her from a long way away – from the library. Could she have been our Rebecca?'

'Hardly.'

'Why not? Where was Rebecca?'

'Outside somewhere, I think. That's right, she was round the side –'

'How do you know?'

'She told me.'

'She could have been in the hall earlier, fled down the far corridor and got out of the building on the east side and then come round to the front.'

'Why – why should she do that?' asked Tish. Whatever was Miss Welbeck getting at? 'I don't think the girl I saw had anything to do with the fire alarm going off, anyway,' she said quickly. 'I'm sure she was a senior.'

'So you accept that it's most unlikely that a senior is the hoaxer?' said Miss Welbeck. 'That theory would not be very sensible, would it?'

'Of course not,' said Tish.

'And you accept that it couldn't be a junior, because no juniors have a half-day on Wednesday and they were all at first lesson –?'

'Yes,' said Tish.

'And therefore our hoaxer is a member of the Middle School,' postulated Miss Welbeck. 'So why are you so certain the girl you saw was a senior?'

'She just was, somehow,' said Tish. She didn't quite follow the logic of all this. 'She was tall –'

'Rebecca Mason is tall. Let's change the subject. Why was Rebecca out of bed at midnight on Sunday?'

'She got up to get a drink, that's all!' said Tish indignantly.

'Where was it, then?' asked Miss Welbeck. 'Mrs Barrington could find no sign of it, afterwards. I did ask her to check, you know.'

'I – I expect she put the glass away,' said Tish. Her mind was getting fuzzy. 'Oh, this is silly –' She remembered something. 'How could Rebecca have rung you? She doesn't know your number, Miss Welbeck. None of us do.'

'I wasn't at my house. I was over at Parkinson. I often am, you know.'

'Oh.' Tish was getting more and more bemused.

'Now to come back to the girl you saw, this afternoon. Can we take it that it was Rebecca? That she was leaning against the wall. Look, like this –'

Miss Welbeck got up and walked over to the wall of her study. She leant against it, on one elbow –

'Yes, that's how the girl was leaning,' said Tish.

'Then suddenly, Rebecca did *this* –' Miss Welbeck made a violent jab at the wall behind her, with her elbow '– in order to smash the emergency glass.'

Tish just shook her head. Suddenly her mind was very, very clear again.

'I'm sorry, Miss Welbeck. The girl might have done that – but it wasn't Rebecca. That's ridiculous. Completely ridiculous!'

Miss Welbeck walked back to her desk, smiled and sat down.

'Very well, Ishbel. You may go.'

Tish walked to the door and took the handle. She turned round. Miss Welbeck was marking some papers, as though she'd already forgotten her existence.

'Will I be punished?' she asked, in a small voice. 'For calling the fire brigade.'

'No,' said Miss Welbeck, without looking up.

Afterwards, Tish had the feeling that the Principal had been having some sort of game with her. But she couldn't be sure.

In spite of the fact that Rebecca and Pippa played badly, and lost, Trebizon got through. Alison and Jilly won their match and then, after some nail-biting suspense, Della and Kate clinched theirs 9–7 in the final set. But Trebizon had come within a hairsbreadth of being knocked out of the cup in the first round!

As Tish put it: 'Miss Dreadful looks it!'

At the tennis tea, the mistress said to Pippa and Rebecca: 'You two had better pull yourselves together before the next round. You've got a fortnight.'

When they saw the Caxton High team off, after tea, there was a general air of ill feeling.

'I can't bear to look at their poor minibus,' said Pippa. 'It's been a dreadful afternoon, hasn't it, Rebecca? And whatever happened to *us*?'

'I don't know,' said Rebecca, helplessly.

'Hadn't you better go and see how your friend Tish got on?' asked Pippa gently. Then she smiled reassuringly. 'I expect everything's all right, Rebecca.'

As Rebecca walked away, she glanced back and saw that Pippa was walking back to Parkinson House, along past the big cedar tree. She remembered that it was Pippa's last term and suddenly she felt sad that this afternoon had marred it for her.

'It's this hoaxing business,' Rebecca thought angrily. 'It's rather horrible. Us getting the blame – Pippa getting upset!'

She sprinted all the way back to Court House and found Tish and the others in the Common Room.

'We've got to find out who the hoaxer is!' they burst out.

'Did you get punished, Tish?' Rebecca asked anxiously.

'No, she let me off,' said Tish. 'But I was given a real grilling, all the same! Miss Welbeck's baffled, if you ask me. She even floated a wild theory that you could be the hoaxer, Rebecca –'

That didn't surprise Rebecca.

'Well, it could have been me, couldn't it? I mean, look at Sunday night. And as for setting off the fire alarm –' Rebecca looked solemn. 'I was on my own, wasn't I? I haven't got an alibi.'

They all looked so worried that she laughed.

'But then, nor have you Tish!'

'And nor have lots of other people!' added Sue.

They started to joke about it then, as a kind of reaction to the tension of the afternoon, suggesting all sorts of unlikely suspects.

'Miss Hort –'

'No, Gatesy –'

But, beneath it all, they were determined to try and find out who the hoaxer really was. If they could.

'Well, you six are good at solving mysteries,' said Robbie, later. He had telephoned to find out how the match had gone. 'I expect you'll find the culprit.'

But he was wrong. This particular mystery looked insoluble.

NINE
A Walk on the Beach with Robbie

At assembly the next morning, Miss Welbeck referred publicly to the matter for the last time:

'There's no need for me to go into the unhappy details of the hoax that was played on the school yesterday afternoon. You all know about it and you also know that this is the second hoax to have been played here within a week. I've one simple message to give the hoaxer. This sort of behaviour cannot be tolerated at Trebizon. I'm thinking about you, all the time, whoever you are. I expect you to come forward and own up. Do not assume from my future silence that I've forgotten this affair. My patience is long. I shall bide my time.'

There was a deathly hush in the big assembly hall.

'Phew,' said Tish, in III Alpha's form room

afterwards. 'The hoaxer must be shaking in her shoes. Bet she doesn't play any more.'

'D'you think she'll own up now?' asked Margot.

'Hope so,' said Elf.

'Well, it's all very well for Miss Welbeck to sit back and wait,' said Rebecca. 'But we're not going to!' She was still angry that the six of them, and she and Tish in particular, were under a cloud of suspicion. A few funny glances as they'd come out of Assembly hadn't escaped her notice. 'We've got to be like real detectives – reconstruct the crimes. Somebody, somewhere, must have seen or heard something suspicious. Either Sunday night, or yesterday afternoon, when the glass panel was smashed –'

'Would you girls at the back please stop talking and go to your desks?' said Miss Hort, their form mistress, who also took them for maths. 'And please stop fiddling with your calculator, Elizabeth, and see if you can use your brain this lesson – exercise it a little.'

Miss Hort was rather brusque, with a crisp line in classroom conversation, but the girls liked her.

'And don't toss your hair back at me, Rebecca Mason, or I'll ask you to have it cut.'

'I was just tossing it out of my eyes, Miss Hort.'

For the rest of that week, the six had the investigating craze. They went around the school questioning people.

Had they seen anybody run out of the main building, just after the fire alarm was set off? Alternatively, had they heard anybody in their boarding house use the phone very late on Sunday night? Did they know anybody who might have a grudge against the school? Or against Miss Welbeck personally?

They followed up various clues. But none of them led anywhere.

'Half of Juniper House seems to have a grudge about something, if Susannah's to be believed,' sighed Margot.

'Mainly about food though, not the right sort, not enough of it,' said Elf, with her plump smile. 'One quite understands that sort of grudge.'

'We know it's not a junior, anyway,' said Sue. 'It'd be impossible for a junior to sneak out of a big dormitory and use the phone at night, without Miss Morgan or somebody knowing –'

'And they were at lessons when the fire bell went,' added Tish.

'Let's face it, we're not getting anywhere,' said Rebecca.

The worst part of it was that some people were beginning to laugh at them while others, like Margaret Exton, put the word around that their activities were all a big cover-up – they were just trying to deflect suspicion from someone amongst their own number.

'Why not just forget it?' Pippa said kindly to Rebecca, after tennis practice on Saturday. 'It doesn't look as though there are going to be any more hoaxes. Think about something pleasant – like the match on the nineteenth! It's a lovely journey to St Mary's – and they've got beautiful courts. We have to make up for last time, Rebecca! We *do* seem to be playing well together now.'

They'd just played a match against Miss Darling and Miss Willis and managed to take a set off them.

Even Miss Darling had said 'Played' and very nearly smiled.

That night, Rebecca, Tish and Sue lay in their beds and took stock of the situation.

'As far as the fire alarm goes, nobody saw a thing and that's that,' said Tish. 'After she'd smashed the panel the girl must have moved like lightning. Fled down a side corridor, I suppose. She certainly didn't come out the front because Della and Jilly and Kate were waiting for the minibus and they didn't see a *thing!*'

'That leaves the phone call last Sunday night,' sighed Sue. 'The girl said she was ringing from Court House, but she wasn't. Rebecca was wide awake and she'd have seen or *heard* if someone had used the phone.'

'Right,' said Rebecca. 'So we know the hoaxer is nobody in Court House.'

'The other boarding house we can rule out completely is Parkinson,' said Sue. 'According to Tish, Miss Welbeck *received* the phone call there. As they've only got one line, nobody could have been *making* the call from there at the same time!'

'Unless Miss Welbeck was phoning herself,' giggled Tish. 'Can't imagine anybody in the Upper Sixth playing hoaxes, anyway. I don't know about you two, but this mystery is getting me cross-eyed.'

'We can rule out everybody in Court House and we can rule out everybody in Parkinson House,' said Rebecca, the most dogged of the three. 'We can also rule out Juniper House. So that narrows it down to –' she ticked the boarding houses off on her fingers '– Norris, Tavistock, Chambers, Sterndale and Willoughby.'

There was silence.

'Not all that narrow, is it?' said Sue, at last.

'No,' admitted Rebecca.

It seemed that that was as far as they were likely to get.

'Maybe we should just forget it?' said Tish.

'That's what Pippa says,' said Rebecca.

It took a while to forget it. But, by the time a week had gone by and she'd played some tennis with the county D squad, it began to fade a little. No more hoaxes were played. By the following week, with the cup match against St Mary's to think about, the whole thing had gone out of Rebecca's mind.

But it hadn't gone out of Miss Welbeck's.

'Do you realise, Evelyn,' she said to the senior maths mistress, 'that it's very nearly a fortnight since the affair of the false fire alarm?'

'You said you might have to bide your time.'

'I'm tired of waiting,' said the Principal unhappily. 'I think I must try and exert a little pressure now.'

For Rebecca, the evening before the match was one of the happiest of the whole term.

It was Tuesday and a beautiful May evening, coming at the end of a sunny day. Tennis practice was kept to half an hour. 'Well done, all of you,' said Miss Darling. 'Now save your strength for the match tomorrow. We're going to win!'

Annie Lorrimer had been waiting for Pippa outside the courts and they went off for a walk through the grounds, arm in arm, heads bent close together. Annie had been very busy lately, doing some important music exams, but these were over and she and Pippa spent a lot of time in each other's company again.

Rebecca felt slightly at a loss. It was too late to go and join the others. They'd gone to Mulberry Cove to meet Curly Watson, Mike Brown and Chris Earl-Smith, their friends in the Third Year at Garth College, for a swim. She came away from south courts, and dawdled. Then she sat down on the grass under the cedar tree. It was cool, lovely! There were faint breezes stirring above. She couldn't bear to return to the boarding house, and go back indoors, not yet . . .

'Rebecca!' Somebody had run silently up behind the tree and now peered round the massive girth of its trunk. 'Found you!'

'Robbie!'

He pulled her up to her feet and she stared at him in surprise. His black curly hair was wild and uncombed and there were rings under his eyes, but he bore himself happily like a small boy playing truant, all six foot of him.

'You're supposed to be studying!' laughed Rebecca.

Tish's brother was in the Fifth Year, with his important GCSEs only three weeks away. He was working very hard, by all accounts.

'It's such a marvellous evening,' smiled Robbie. 'I decided to break free for an hour! Besides, I want to talk to you. Come for a walk?'

They went down to the bay and walked across the sands together, slowly, while Robbie gave Rebecca a long lecture about the match the next day. He knew what had happened at the previous match and he didn't want it to happen again.

'Concentration is the only thing that really matters,' he told her. 'While you're playing you've got to watch that ball the whole time and shut out the rest of the world, so that it doesn't even exist. It doesn't matter what's happened just before the match, or what's going to happen just after, shut it all out . . . play every single point as though *that* were the one that decides the game.'

Quite suddenly, he put his arm round her shoulders.

'Don't let yourself down, will you, Rebeck?'

'I'll try not to,' said Rebecca. She suddenly felt confident.

He dropped his arm and walked her back to Court House, in silence. Finally, outside the front porch, he said:

'Is it true you've been given a fantastic new dress for Commem?'

'Yes!' said Rebecca. The dress had been tucked away at the back of the clothes cupboard, ever since the county tennis party. 'I wonder what Commem's like?'

Commemoration Day was at the end of June and was held in honour of the school's founder. A special service took place in the morning and in the evening was the Commem Ball. This year Rebecca and her friends would be allowed to go to the Ball, which was for the Middle School and upwards, only.

'I don't know,' said Robbie. 'Why don't you let me take you and then we can find out.'

Rebecca stared at him.

'What's the matter? Have you got a partner already?'

Rebecca shook her head. She'd never even thought about partners.

'*Will* you, then?'

'I – I'll have to find out what the others are doing,' said Rebecca, looking confused.

'Well, Tish has said she'll go with Edward. I know that for a fact.'

'The dark horse!' thought Rebecca.

'Will you?'

'Yes.'

'*Good!*' He looked pleased. '*Excellent*, in fact!'

That was a moment when Rebecca felt especially happy.

Sixteen schools had entered for the inter-schools cup and now Trebizon was in the last eight. If they beat St Mary's, they'd go through to the semi-final. The match against St Mary's was an away match and it was too far for Trebizon's supporters to come and cheer. In fact, it was quite a long train journey away and the team would be having lunch on the train. In case a substitute were suddenly needed, so far from home, Lady Edwina was going to travel with the team as reserve.

On Wednesday morning, not long before the team was due to catch its train from Trebizon station, Miss Welbeck called Pippa to her study.

'Pippa, I'm sorry to have to involve you again. It's rather unpleasant, but I feel you can be a great help to me.'

'Unpleasant?' Pippa jumped slightly. 'I don't understand, Miss Welbeck.'

'You're quite close to Rebecca Mason, aren't you? She thinks a great deal of you. When you come back on the train this evening, after the match, would you sit with her? Talk to her?'

'*Talk* to her –?'

'Yes, if anyone can persuade her to own up, I'm sure you can. You see, Pippa, I'm perfectly certain in my own mind that Rebecca is our little hoaxer. My patience is wearing rather thin. But I want her to come forward of her own free will.'

Pippa stood there. She looked stunned. Her mouth opened and closed but no sound came out.

'Off you go and get ready then,' said Miss Welbeck, briskly. 'We can't have you missing the train.'

TEN
A Bad Day for Pippa

Pippa was very quiet on the train. She seemed really fed up. And when they played their match against St Mary's third pair, her mind simply wasn't on tennis.

She missed some shots, overhit others. Her forehand, usually a winner, kept going into the top of the net. She just couldn't seem to concentrate.

'Take more of the play, Rebecca,' whispered Miss Darling, in some anguish, when they'd lost the first set 1-6. 'Jilly and Alison are getting beaten, too. You've *got* to win this match!'

It very nearly unnerved Rebecca, the way Pippa was playing. But then she remembered Robbie's advice yesterday: . . . *shut out the rest of the world, so that it doesn't exist.* Today, *the rest of the world* meant even her own partner!

She shut Pippa out and just played her own game, running for everything, volleying and smashing and intercepting in marvellous form – and they took the second set 6–3.

But by the final set she was tiring. It was exhausting, one person trying to cover a doubles court! The opposition was playing more and more to Pippa and Pippa still couldn't find her touch. Somehow, by Rebecca hanging on grimly with some inspired play, they managed to level at six games all.

She needed a home crowd, to lift her, but all the shouting was for St Mary's. Della and Kate won. Jilly and Alison had lost. So it was 1–1 and this match was the decider. If they went down now, Trebizon were out of the cup!

St Mary's served some double faults in the next game and by almost running herself into the ground on a long rally, Rebecca managed to take the game for her and Pippa. They were leading 7–6!

But Rebecca was on the very brink of exhaustion. As she towelled her face down by the umpire's chair and took a quick drink she said to Miss Darling:

'That last rally finished me. I don't think I can run any more.'

'Then *serve*, Rebecca. It's your service. Beat them

on service.'

Rebecca's legs were giving out beneath her, but her arms were still strong. She thought of everything Robbie had taught her – he'd taught her to serve like he did – hard, unstoppable, swerving services. Could she produce some now? It was the only way to end the agony!

Because if she let it go to 7–7, with their best server to come, that would be the end.

She served. It was an ace!

Then another!

'Thirty love,' said the umpire.

Rebecca closed her eyes. Play every single point as though it's the one that decides the game.

Another good service; this time it came back in a limp sky-high lob –

Pippa moved up to the net. She couldn't possibly miss that one!

'Forty love.'

Three match points.

A beautiful deep service – a good return to Rebecca's forehand – Rebecca got it back – then it came back on the far side of the court. It was no good, she couldn't run another step. But Pippa was moving up to the ball –

Crack!

It was a winner!

'Game, set and match to Trebizon.'

Rebecca nearly fainted with relief. Sportingly, the onlookers applauded.

'Did you see the way that kid played?' someone said.

'She deserved to win, playing on her own like that!'

'Well done, Rebecca!'

The team crowded round her, clapping her on the back.

But what was wrong with Pippa?

She was quiet all through the tennis tea, moody even. There was an air of secret anticipation about Eddie Burton, who'd sat on the sidelines as reserve and been forced to watch Pippa's poor play with mounting frustration. And Eddie was right to be hopeful.

Miss Darling looked grim.

'Were you feeling all right this afternoon?' she asked Pippa on the train journey back to Trebizon. 'You played very badly.'

'I'm sorry.' Pippa shrugged. 'Just one of those things.'

'Worried about exams? Working too hard?' Pippa was taking A levels after half-term. But then so were Della, Kate and Jilly.

'No harder than anybody else,' said Pippa. 'I don't believe in making excuses. I just played badly. Rebecca played well, thank goodness.'

'I've had a word with Kate and we think Eddie had better come in for the semi-final,' Miss Darling said then. 'She hasn't got any big exams this term.'

Pippa leaned back against the carriage seat and closed her eyes for a moment. Dropped from the team! She must have played badly!

'Whatever you and Kate think best,' she said.

She opened her eyes and stared out at fields and woods, flashing by, without even seeing them. She was still sitting like that when the train pulled in at Trebizon station.

'We're here, Pippa,' whispered Rebecca.

Pippa had been dropped from the team – just like that! Rebecca could still hardly take it in. And this was her last term!

But she was sure there was something else on Pippa's mind – and she kept wondering what it was.

She never dreamt that it was to do with her.

As soon as they got back to school, Pippa went to see Miss Welbeck.

'I haven't spoken to Rebecca,' she said. There was a high colour in her cheeks. 'I didn't think it was necessary!'

'You didn't?'

'I'm perfectly certain that Rebecca had nothing to do with the hoaxes!'

'Oh?' Miss Welbeck sounded sceptical.

'Why – why would a girl like Rebecca behave like that?' Pippa burst out. 'What are your reasons for thinking it was her?'

'I don't have to explain my reasons to you, Philippa.'

'But – but you must have some –'

'Oh, she's at a silly age, you know.'

Pippa felt as though she must leave the room before she exploded. She took a few paces towards the door, then stopped, and turned round.

'If you're so sure it's Rebecca, why don't you have her in and ask her, outright? You'll soon find out you've got the wrong girl!'

'I wouldn't dream of doing such a thing,' Miss Welbeck said, icily.

'But you've had other people in!' Pippa exclaimed.

'I'm handling things differently now,' said Miss Welbeck.

ELEVEN
The Taxi Driver Remembers

Right up to half-term, things went marvellously well for Rebecca. In so many ways this term, which she would always look back to as the tennis term, was turning out to be the best ever.

Why couldn't it be like that for Pippa?

After she was dropped from the team, Pippa seemed to withdraw.

'It's probably for the best,' she told Rebecca, the morning after they'd been to St Mary's. 'I've always said you were going to leave me far behind at tennis, haven't I? Besides, my exams are next month and now I'll have more time to work.'

But Rebecca knew that she was just putting a brave face on things. It had been humiliating to play so badly and be dropped from the team. And there was something else worrying her, too, a lurking uneasiness just below the surface. She saw very little of Pippa over the next two weeks but sometimes she caught glimpses of it in her face. Rebecca decided it must be to do with the exams. Poor Pippa! She'd never thought of her as the anxious sort.

Rebecca herself was finding life wonderful.

The second half of May was glorious and she went swimming and surfing in Trebizon Bay several times. The Third Year boys from Garth College joined them sometimes and they were such fun to be with! She saw nothing of Robbie, still slaving away for his Fifth Year exams, but she looked forward (with a secret glow of anticipation) to the Commem Ball at the end of June and to wearing her new dress.

She played in another round-robin tournament, organised for the county C and D junior squads, and did very well. 'You're in the running for promotion if you keep this up, Rebecca,' Mrs Ericson told her.

Most heartening of all, the whole business of the hoaxes seemed to have been forgotten. It looked like being one of the world's great unsolved mysteries. The unpleasant little shadow of suspicion that had clung round Rebecca and Tish had faded away and

Rebecca now seemed very popular, for the news of how she'd played at St Mary's had quickly spread round the school. The baby of the team had saved the day!

The Trebizon girls were a competitive lot and they loved winning. Now they were in the semi-final of the inter-schools cup!

It was thus expected and demanded of the First VI that they beat Hillstone School and get to the final.

On Wednesday, second of June, they did just that! It was an away match at the rival school, which was in the centre of the big town of Hillstone, some forty miles away. The Trebizon team scored a convincing win – 3-0 – and Miss Darling was actually seen to smile! Rebecca had missed Pippa badly at team practices, finding Eddie Burton a very stolid and unexciting partner by comparison, but there was no doubt that Eddie proved rock-like on the day, with none of the alarming unpredictability that Pippa had displayed on the day of the St Mary's match.

The news swept around the school and when, the following morning, Miss Welbeck announced at Assembly that the final would be played at Trebizon

on the afternoon of Saturday, twenty-sixth June –
the school's Commemoration Day – cup fever
reached a new pitch.

'That might be quite a day for you, Rebecca,' said
Sue. Rebecca had told the others her secret now –
that Robbie would be taking her to the Commem
Ball.

'It's the Garth College tennis cup that day and
Robbie usually wins it!' realised Tish. 'Just think – if
he wins and you win –' She giggled. 'It'll be just like
the Wimbledon Ball!' She pushed Rebecca into the
form room, where Miss Gerard was waiting to take
them for French. 'Pity he's such a rotten dancer!'

Rebecca laughed. But all through French she
kept going off into little daydreams.

'Pay attention, Monique!' exclaimed Miss Gerard.

Rebecca wondered who Monique was and then
suddenly remembered that was her French name!

They broke up for half-term on Friday afternoon –
after Sports Day.

Tish won the intermediate 800 metres and
both Aba and Laura broke records in the sprints.
All three girls qualified for the area sports. Unlike
last Sports Day, the weather had suddenly turned
cool and cloudy and so the special tea took place

in the dining hall, instead of out-of-doors on the terrace. But the little sandwiches and sausage rolls and coffee cake and cream eclairs were as delicious as ever.

Mr and Mrs Murdoch were there with Sue's brothers David and Edward – Garth College had broken up at lunch time – and so were all the Andersons. They included Rebecca in everything and Robbie was especially attentive – so much so that Doctor Anderson looked at his wife and raised his eyebrows. Nevertheless it was at times like this that Rebecca missed her parents most – and also longed to have a brother or sister and not be an only child.

After tea, she hurried over to the boarding house to collect her weekend case, as the Andersons had offered to drive her to the Bus Station. She was spending half-term at her grandmother's bungalow in Gloucestershire.

Pippa's car was parked outside Court House and Annie was sitting in it. Pippa was waiting for Rebecca in the hall, holding a package.

'Six advance copies of the magazine have just arrived,' she told Rebecca. 'I thought you might like one to send to your parents.'

She took a pristine copy of the summer issue of *The Trebizon Journal* out of the opened package and gave it to Rebecca. It was fresh from the printers and she could still smell the ink.

'It's beautiful!' exclaimed Rebecca. 'Oh, Pippa, your painting's beautiful! The colours –'

She stared at the cover of *The Journal*. Pippa's painting of the cedar tree, with the tiny figure in tennis whites lying beneath it, had made the most stunning cover she'd ever seen on the school magazine! And there, across the foot of the painting, was Rebecca's own poem, set in a decorative panel. Rebecca just stared at it.

'Do you think your parents will like it –?'

'Oh, Pippa!'

Outside, Annie sounded the horn. Pippa was dropping her room-mate off at the station to catch a train to London before driving home to Bristol herself, and they were running late.

'I must dash,' said Pippa, her face clouding over. There was something she wanted to ask Rebecca. She started to back away. But – she must know!

'By the way, Rebecca –'

'Yes?' Rebecca tore her eyes from the cover.

'Have you seen Miss Welbeck yet?'

'Seen Miss Welbeck?' asked Rebecca, puzzled. 'What about?'

'Oh nothing.' Pippa was at once covered in confusion. Outside, the horn sounded again. 'I thought she might have seen you about – but, oh it's nothing important! I must go! Bye, Rebecca.'

' Bye, Pippa.'

What would Miss Welbeck want to see her about? wondered Rebecca. About the poem, maybe? To say something nice about it. Was that what Pippa meant? What was wrong with Pippa these days? She seemed so nervy, somehow.

Rebecca's gaze turned to the magazine cover. Her eyes drank in the dark green of the cedar tree and the golden sunlight. Her mind went right back to the beginning of term, when she'd first seen Pippa start work on the painting.

Pippa had been so happy at the beginning of term. She'd talked about it being her last term, how she wanted it to be perfect, the best ever.

Yet things had gone wrong for her and Rebecca didn't quite know why. It had all started with the hoaxes somehow, that quarrel with Alison, Pippa taking it so much to heart. But of course it couldn't be anything to do with that! It was just that for some reason Pippa wasn't happy any longer and wasn't even quite herself.

Rebecca looked at the picture again and felt saddened.

She spent three quiet days with her grandmother, who lived on a small estate in what was known as a 'retirement area', in a small town in Gloucestershire.

'Lovely to see you, Becky! I've missed you!'

'I've missed you, too, Gran!' She hugged her. 'I haven't seen you for ages!'

'Did that Greek family look after you properly in the Easter holidays?'

'Of course they did, Gran!' Rebecca smiled. 'Their cooking wasn't a patch on yours, though. But, you'll never guess – they bought me a dress! The most lovely, lovely dress –' She described it. 'I've already worn it to a party and I'm going to wear it to the Commem Ball!'

'Nobody else will have a dress like that, I'm quite sure!' said old Mrs Mason. 'What a pity you couldn't have brought it with you to show me – but there, it would have got all squashed up in your little case.'

'It's packed right away at the back of the clothes cupboard,' sighed Rebecca.

Her grandmother exclaimed over the cover of *The Trebizon Journal* and Rebecca's poem. She exclaimed again when she heard about the county tennis and the school team and the inter-schools cup.

Rebecca had brought back enough news to keep her going for weeks!

But she didn't tell her about the hoaxes. They were a thing of the past now. There didn't seem much point.

Even Miss Welbeck had almost given up.

Over half-term she went out to dinner with Colonel Peters, a very old friend who lived in the town, and asked his advice.

'Really, Madeleine, it boils down to whether Mrs Tarkus is a reliable source of information or not. You've only her word for it that one of your girls was mixed up in that dreadful nonsense. You say she can't describe the girl's face or anything like that. Just *sounded* like a Trebizon girl and she was shouting something about getting back to school –'

'And it *was* nearly midnight, George, and we *are* the only girls' boarding school around here –'

'She could have meant she had to get back because she had school the next morning,' pointed out Colonel Peters. 'A Sunday night, wasn't it? Or she could simply have been one of your domestic staff – or Garth's – a few of them live in.'

'True,' said Miss Welbeck. 'Mrs Tarkus seemed so sure . . .'

'She's always sure! A nuisance. A busybody! Always ringing people up late at night and complaining about something or other. She'd like to see the town cleared of young people – completely cleared. Banned!'

Miss Welbeck smiled and shook her head.

But it was the dress that really worried her.

'She described it so graphically.'

'Coincidence!' snorted Colonel Peters. He leaned across the table and touched his companion's hand. 'Look here, Madeleine, discount Mrs Tarkus completely. She's unreliable. Discount her, and what are you left with?'

Miss Welbeck sighed.

'Just – just a couple of very stupid pranks, I suppose,' she admitted.

Rebecca travelled back from her grandmother's on the following Tuesday and her coach arrived at Trebizon Bus Station on the Tuesday afternoon. When she got into the first of three waiting taxis, she found it was her favourite cab driver.

'It's the princess herself!' he said with a broad grin. 'Trebizon School?' As they drove up to the top of the High Street, he gave her a broad wink over his shoulder. 'D'you know, I've been looking out for you for weeks.'

'Oh?' said Rebecca, in surprise.

There was something quite conspiratorial about his manner.

'D'you know you left your scarf in my cab that night?'

'What scarf?' thought Rebecca. 'What night is he talking about?'

'I was going to bring it up to the school for you, but when I read about it in the local paper, I thought I'd better not. Didn't want to get you into trouble!'

Rebecca's mouth was hanging open with curiosity. He'd got her mixed up with somebody else!

'Read about it in the local paper –?' she inquired.

'That rowdy party! The police being called in! That's where you'd been, eh? I wondered what you'd been up to! No wonder you were in such a panic when you waved me down –' They were coming out of the town now and passing the phone box on the top road. 'Right here, it was,' he chuckled. 'You'd just been trying to phone through and then you saw me! I've never seen anyone so pleased to see a taxi as you were that night, me dear. Didn't get caught, did you?'

'Me?' said Rebecca. 'Er–no.'

Rebecca had a remarkably good memory and now she remembered that a noisy party had been going on, in a house called The Lodge across the street from Fenners, on the Sunday she'd got her place in the tennis team. Some time afterwards she'd read somewhere that there'd been a disturbance in the town that night, windows smashed and some youths arrested.

But that had been the day *after* the county tennis party at Exonford, when Rebecca had used the taxi. The cab driver was getting her mixed up with someone else! Why? It must have been someone who looked like her. It was late at night . . . dark. Someone who'd been at the party . . . stepped out of the phone box, panic-stricken, and waved down the taxi to get her back to school. And she'd left her scarf in the taxi.

'Where's the scarf now?' asked Rebecca, her heart beating hard.

'Don't worry, it's down at the office, waiting for you. It's wrapped up in a brown paper parcel. If you can tell me your name, I'll label it for you and you can collect it any time –'

'Rebecca Mason. Yes, write that on, please!'

They were turning in through the school gates.

Rebecca was thinking hard. It looked bad for her, a taxi driver thinking she'd been at a wild party late at night. But the minute she got her hands on that scarf, she'd find out who it belonged to – find out who the girl *really* was.

And that girl – surely – must be the hoaxer?

Why had she played the hoax? Maybe to create a diversion at Court House that night so that she could get back to her *own* house, unseen!

The whole unpleasant business of the hoaxes came back to Rebecca's mind. 'Will I have something to say to her!' she thought. 'Who is she?'

She must get the scarf – quickly!

'Can I come and get it after tea?' she asked. 'What time does the taxi office shut?'

'We're open till seven. I'll write your name on the parcel as soon as I get back, then any of the lads can give it to you. Where you to, now?' he asked, slowing down in the school grounds, unable to remember her boarding house.

They were passing quite close to Parkinson House and Rebecca saw that Pippa was back. Her car was parked outside!

'It's all right, drop me here!' she said. She'd tell Pippa all about it. Pippa could drive her down town to the taxi office, straight after tea!

She paid off the cab driver.

Looking at her face, he was reminded how young she was.

'You'd no business being there that night, mind,'

he said. 'Not mixed up with that crowd any more are you?'

'No, of course not!' exclaimed Rebecca. Then she remembered to smile. 'Thanks,' she said. 'Thanks for everything.'

She raced across to Parkinson House, her weekend case bobbing at her side. Pippa, Annie and Della were making cheese on toast in the kitchen. Pippa looked startled to see Rebecca in the Upper Sixth boarding house and shunted her outside, into the back garden.

'What is it?'

Breathlessly, Rebecca told her everything. Annie appeared at the kitchen door, buttering a piece of toast. 'What's going on?'

'Nothing!' Pippa called.

She turned to Rebecca.

'I'll bring the car to Court House straight after tea, and drive you down there.' She looked uneasy. 'But - caution, Rebecca! Don't tell anybody about this - not till we get a good look at this scarf -'

Rebecca raced away. 'Thanks, Pippa!' Not tell anyone? - she must be mad! Not tell the others? This was the big breakthrough! The mystery they thought could never be solved was about to be cracked!

In about one hour's time they should be able to find out the identity of the hoaxer!

'What's going on?' asked Annie again, coming out into the garden. Pippa was just standing there, watching Rebecca until she was out of sight, a strange expression on her face. Then she turned and looked at Annie and told her.

Annie said: 'Crumbs! Rebecca Mason? The taxi driver thinks it was her?'

'Yes,' replied Pippa.

TWELVE
A Horrible Suspicion!

Even as Rebecca reached her room in Court House, the tea bell sounded. She flung her case on to the bed and linked arms with the other two.

'Come on, let's get over to the dining hall. I've got something to tell you!'

They couldn't stop talking about it, all through tea. People at nearby tables noticed that there was something up at Tish Anderson's table – a lot of whispering and flushed faces – and Rebecca Mason seemed to be the centre of attention.

'I'm going to ring Syon and tell Curly!' said Mara.

'I think I'll tell Robbie, too,' said Tish. 'He was asking me about the hoaxes only today – on the train.'

'Ssssh!' said Rebecca. 'We don't want people to

hear! Once we've got hold of the scarf, we've got to track down the hoaxer and take her by surprise.'

She bolted her tea down and left the dining hall early, running all the way back to Court House. Pippa was already there waiting. She was sitting behind the wheel of her car, which was parked outside the deserted boarding house. Good old Pippa! *She* must be dying to know who the hoaxer was, too. It had certainly upset her a lot when Alison had accused Rebecca's crowd.

'Okay?' said Pippa, starting up the engine.

They drove to the town, in silence. There was an almost electric tension in the air.

'Pippa *is* wondering!' thought Rebecca. 'She wants to know, too!'

She jumped out of the car outside the taxi office and rushed in. One of the cab drivers was in there, taking a phone booking, and she pointed excitedly to the brown paper parcel on a shelf behind his head. It was now clearly marked with her name. He reached up a hand, took it down, and handed it to her while still speaking into the phone. 'Grand Hotel, Exonford? Right.'

'Thanks!' said Rebecca and rushed out.

She looked round for the car and saw that Pippa

had parked across the street, in a quiet place beneath some trees. She went over and got back in the front seat, next to Pippa. 'I've got the scarf – it's in here!'

'Better open it then,' said Pippa.

Fingers shaking slightly, Rebecca undid the string and opened up the wrapping. The material was very soft and blue. There seemed to be long white fringes on it –

'It doesn't look like a scarf, somehow,' she began. A tingling sensation ran down her back. It looked familiar. 'It –' She began to open it out. 'He said a scarf. But – but he meant a stole!' She gasped. 'Mine!'

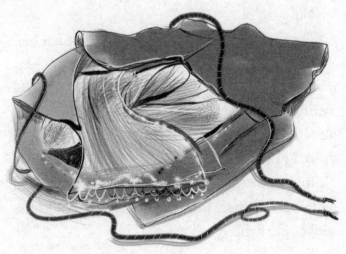

Pippa glanced at the stole, looked at Rebecca

strangely and then reached out to turn the ignition key.

'What a let-down!' she said, casually.

'But –' Rebecca was totally perplexed.

'It's obvious, isn't it?' Pippa said. 'Silly man got confused. You left your stole in his taxi after you'd been to Exonford. Must have done. Then he had this other passenger the next night – he's got the two of you mixed up in his mind.'

'But *why*?' exclaimed Rebecca. 'Why on earth should he do that?'

'Must have done!' Pippa started the engine. 'Better forget it.'

'No!'

Pippa switched off the engine and looked at her.

'I *didn't* leave my stole in his taxi on the Saturday evening!' protested Rebecca. 'I *know* I didn't. I was wearing it when I got back to Court House and I hung it up in the back of the cupboard, with the dress, I'm sure I did.'

'But you couldn't have done,' said Pippa, nodding. 'It's here. Right here. It was found in the taxi! Look, Rebecca –'

'Yes?'

Pippa was glancing at her very oddly now and

suddenly Rebecca felt the tension again. It was hanging in the air, between them.

'Look, you'd better not go around saying you had your stole when you got back on the Saturday night. I mean, it's going to look bad for you if you go around saying that! People are going to think you were out again on the Sunday night – I mean, the taxi driver seems to think you were!'

'Yes,' said Rebecca. Her throat felt dry. It could look like that!

Pippa switched on the engine again and this time she drove the car away.

'You've just got muddled, Rebecca! You're as bad as him!'

Rebecca said nothing. There was something very peculiar going on. She couldn't understand it. She simply *couldn't* understand it!

As they drove up to the front of Court House, quite a crowd burst out – Tish and Sue and the other three – and Curly – and Robbie as well. 'Rebecca!' they all cried, starting to run towards the car.

'You've told all your friends!' Pippa said sharply. 'Rebecca – I warned you! Put it back in the brown paper, quickly.'

Guiltily, Rebecca hid the stole inside the brown

paper, rolling it up tightly. 'What shall I say?'

'Get them inside, or something. I'll explain to them about the muddle –'

Robbie was opening the car door and pulling Rebecca out.

'Tish told me; I came straight over! Let's see this scarf –'

'Just a minute, Robbie – *I* want to see something!' she exclaimed.

While Pippa parked the car, Rebecca hurtled past Robbie and the others and raced into the boarding house, the brown paper parcel held tightly under her arm. She rushed through the hall, round into the little corridor and into her room. She opened the hanging cupboard and rummaged all through the clothes until she could feel her dress at the back. She jerked it out, still on its hanger. She let the brown paper parcel slip to the floor.

The stole should have been wrapped round the hanger, inside the dress. That was how she'd left it, surely? Four – five weeks ago.

It wasn't there. Just the dress.

'Where's the stole?' asked Tish, coming into the room quickly. Robbie was just behind her. He pointed to the floor.

'That it?'

The wrappings had fallen apart and a mass of blue material with white fringes peeped out. Rebecca scooped the bundle up, guiltily, paper as well – furious with herself because she could feel herself blushing. The others were all pressing into the room now, Sue first, followed by Curly Watson with his arm round Mara's shoulders.

'What's going on?' asked Robbie, frowning. 'I thought this girl was in the taxi. The one who'd been to The Lodge. But that's your *own* scarf thing, you've brought back –'

'Stole,' Tish corrected him, automatically.

There was quite a crowd in the corridor now, trying to see what was going on in the room. Pippa pushed her way through, came into the room and closed the door.

'Look, this is embarrassing for Rebecca, so I'd better explain! I'm afraid she's got you all excited about nothing. It's just a mix-up! The cab driver found Rebecca's stole in his cab from the day before and somehow he thought it was this other girl's . . . that's all. Look, break it up now. Boys aren't supposed to come into the rooms –'

She opened the door, in a hurry to be gone.

'Clear off, you lot! It's nothing. Shoo!' Everybody scattered as the prefect walked out into the corridor, waving her arms, and then left.

'Phew,' said Robbie. He stared at the stole in Rebecca's hands, in relief. Outside, Rebecca could hear the faint sound of Pippa's car engine starting up.

'But, I don't get it,' murmured Tish, frowning.

'Nor do I,' said Sue.

It was Elf who blurted it out. She just couldn't help herself.

'You *didn't* leave it in the taxi: You were wearing it, Rebecca!'

'Round your head,' added Margot. 'You looked lovely!'

Robbie stared at Rebecca. Mara rolled her eyes in dismay.

'Were you?' he asked.

'Yes,' said Rebecca.

'So you were in the taxi *again*, the following night?' he exclaimed. 'You went to that party? Who on earth took you to that?'

'Don't be silly, Robbie –' began Sue.

'Don't act as if you own Rebecca!' said Tish angrily.

'Did you all go?' Curly asked suddenly. He looked at Mara suspiciously. 'When we weren't allowed to have a bit of a party here! *Did you all go down there?*'

The house known as The Lodge was notorious at Garth College – and strictly out of bounds. There'd been too many bad parties there.

'Oh, Curly!' Mara was shocked. 'Of course we didn't.'

'We all stayed here,' said Tish. 'Rebecca as well.'

'How do you know she did?' asked Robbie. Suddenly he stepped forward and took hold of Rebecca's wrists.

'Who took you to that place?'

'*Let me go!*' She pulled herself free. 'Nobody!'

'You did go somewhere, didn't you? It *is* your stole, isn't it?'

Curly steered Mara out of the room, and her room-mates followed.

'Come on, Robbie!' said Tish, jocularly grabbing his arm. 'Time to go! Exams tomorrow. Leave Rebecca alone –'

'Who took you there?' said Robbie again, in a fury.

'Go away!' shouted Rebecca. '*Please go away!*'

The other two started pushing him out of the

room. 'Okay. Okay. I'm going,' he said miserably. He glanced back at Rebecca, who'd sat down on her bed, still holding the stole. 'I'm sorry, Rebeck . . .'

He just didn't know what to think.

'I'm not going to the Commem with you!' she flung at him. 'I'd rather not go at all!'

Tish and Sue saw him off at the front door. Court House was buzzing with rumour – Rebecca Mason was the hoaxer!

When they returned to the room, Rebecca was stretched full length on her bed, staring up at the ceiling.

'He's still wondering if you could have slipped off to that party with someone for a couple of hours,' said Tish awkwardly. 'After we were all asleep. Got a bit silly and played that hoax maybe –'

'He's only wondering,' said Sue, pushing her glasses up. She couldn't take her eyes off the stole, now draped across the foot of Rebecca's bed.

'He's not the only one, is he?' said Rebecca, in a flat voice. 'Did I sound the fire alarm, too? Like Miss Welbeck said?'

'Come on, Sue,' said Tish. 'You'll be late for music practice.'

Rebecca knew that, right at this very moment,

even her two best friends were shaken. But what could she say to reassure them? How could she explain it? It was all so very, very peculiar.

For Rebecca, it was a low point.

But as soon as he got back to Garth College, Robbie phoned her.

'Rebecca, I'm sorry. I was stupid, thinking those things about you! The things you think in the heat of the moment!' He sounded excited. 'I've been racking my brains, all the way back. It's come to me! Somebody must have *borrowed* your stole that night! Somebody from *Parkinson House!*'

'Parkinson?' said Rebecca, in amazement.

'Look, as I cycled out of your grounds, I took a look at the geography. Court House is just about the farthest possible point away from Parkinson –'

'Yes?'

'Well, Miss Welbeck was in *Parkinson* when she took the call. Somebody sent her chasing off on a wild goose chase to *Court!* Why –?'

'To draw her off, so they could get back into Parkinson!' exclaimed Rebecca. 'Of course! I'd got as far as thinking the hoax might have been intended to divert attention from one of the other Middle

School houses, but –'

'No! Parkinson!' repeated Robbie.

'I'm going over there right now!' said Rebecca, suddenly as excited as he was.

'Pippa will help me! I've got to convince her that the cab driver *didn't* get in a muddle – and then she'll help me find out who was really in his taxi that night!

'Oh, Robbie!' she added. 'Thank goodness *somebody* believes me.'

'You didn't mean what you said about Commem?'

'Yes!' Rebecca paused, then smiled. 'But I've changed my mind.'

THIRTEEN
Unravelling The Mystery

'Pippa will help me!' Rebecca thought again. 'As soon as I tell her that the others – *all* of them – remember me wearing the stole when I got back from Exonford, she'll have to accept that I *didn't* leave it in the taxi that Saturday!'

Somebody else wore it on the Sunday! Who?

Rebecca had fetched the stole and put it around her shoulders. The evening was cool now.

She made her way through the grounds.

Parkinson House was a pleasant Victorian house, rather like a vicarage, set in its own garden. As it came in sight, it occurred to Rebecca that there was one fatal weakness in Robbie's theory. Was it really likely that a mighty member of the Upper Sixth would have ransacked her room and borrowed her stole for a night out?

Wasn't that rather an extraordinary idea? Would Pippa – even Pippa – believe it? If Tish and Sue, her closest friends, were a little bit shaken by the whole thing – wouldn't Pippa be, too?

As she turned in through the side gate, Rebecca's courage almost failed her. She walked up to the side door and hovered there, then suddenly came to a decision.

She had absolute faith in Pippa. She was the only person left she could turn to!

She opened the door.

She'd never been to Pippa's rooms before, but she knew that they were on the first floor, at the front. She'd seen her at the windows sometimes, gazing out. She'd go straight up there!

She tiptoed along the hall and scuttled past the Common Room, glancing towards the wide staircase. She didn't particularly want her presence to be noticed. It gave her a creepy feeling to think that *somebody*, here in this building, must be the guilty person. That *they* had worn this stole she was wearing now – and left it in the taxi that night! She passed by the telephone at the bottom of the stairs. *That* was where the call had come through, the call taken by Miss Welbeck.

She took the stairs lightly, two at a time, reached the first floor landing and turned right. The boards creaked as she walked along the landing – which was the door – that one there?

She tiptoed up and saw the name-card: *P. Fellowes-Walker & A. Lorrimer.*

She could hear a stereo playing inside; it was classical music and on loud.

Rebecca knocked.

No reply.

'Pippa?' she called in a low voice.

Still no response.

Pippa must be in there, perhaps in the farthest room! She wouldn't hear someone knocking, because of the stereo. Rebecca stood there helplessly, wondering what to do. She was so keyed up. She couldn't bear to turn round and go away again, having got this far.

Shyly, she edged the door open and peered inside. This must be Annie's room. It was empty. The stereo was in here and sheet music was strewn around; a violin case lay on a divan. But at the far end of the room, another room led off – that would be Pippa's. Its door was half-open.

Pippa must be in here.

Rebecca walked through Annie's room and called:

'Pippa!'

'Annie?' asked Pippa, from somewhere within.

Then, in a rush came the words, 'Don't worry, I'm going to send it home. I wish I'd sent it home on the very first day of term! If only I had! If only you hadn't stopped me! How do I look –?'

'It's me!' began Rebecca, stepping into the room.

She froze.

Pippa twirled towards her, eyes closed and arms outstretched, wearing a beautiful dress and matching stole, a shimmer of blue swirling skirt and whirling white fringes –

'My dress!' said Rebecca, hoarsely.

'Rebecca!' Pippa's eyes opened wide.

They stood staring at one another. Rebecca held up her arm and looked at the fringes of the stole she was wearing – then she looked at the one Pippa was wearing. It was like seeing a mirror image.

'What are you doing here?' said Pippa in a surprised voice.

A chill ran through Rebecca. 'I – I –' She took a step back.

'You never said you had a dress like mine!' she burst out.

'No.'

Rebecca began to shiver, as though with cold. Words started to echo in her brain, Pippa's sharp words earlier. *You've told all your friends!* That hadn't seemed quite right at the time. Why shouldn't she have told all her friends? And – *Rebecca, I warned you!* What was there for Pippa to warn her about?

Unless Pippa had known all along exactly what

was going to be inside that brown paper parcel at the taxi office.

'You –' Rebecca swallowed hard. There could only be one explanation! 'You went in my room today and took my stole! While Court House was empty. While we were over in the dining hall, having tea!'

'Yes.'

'When you drove me to the taxi office you had it in the car with you – hidden somewhere. You'd just been in and got it! And that's it – you're wearing it now. The one I'm wearing –' She ran her fingers through the fringes, still stupefied. 'The one I'm wearing is *yours*. It was your stole that was left in the taxi.'

'That's correct, Rebecca.'

The stereo was still playing at full volume.

Hot tears welled up in Rebecca's eyes. 'Then you were the hoaxer, all along!'

She wanted to hear Pippa deny it, but Pippa was silent.

Rebecca kept shaking her head. She was dumbfounded.

'If somebody like you can't be trusted,' she said, 'then who –?'

'Rebecca!' Gently Pippa put an arm round Rebecca's shoulders. She was close to tears herself. Really, the strain of it all had been too much! 'For goodness' sake don't *cry*. There's nothing to cry about!'

Suddenly Rebecca heard somebody else's voice.

Annie Lorrimer had been standing outside the door for a full minute, horror struck. Now she stepped into the room.

She looked awful.

'It's no good, is it?' she said. 'It didn't work, after all. I think I'd better go and see Miss Welbeck.'

'Annie - you'll lose everything!' said Pippa, in anguish.

'Maybe I deserve to,' she said.

Annie! Annie Lorrimer was the hoaxer!

What a story Rebecca had to tell the others!

Pippa had bought the dress in the Easter holidays, for her last Commem Ball, but finding out that Rebecca had the identical dress, she'd sadly packed her own away. It would be too unkind to Rebecca to wear it now!

It was the kid's first Commem - her first good dress, maybe. She probably thought it was unique.

Pippa had wanted to send hers home, but Annie begged her not to. She loved going to parties and borrowing Pippa's dresses when she got tired of her own. Maybe she could wear it just once, at some occasion out of school.

Like one of those forbidden parties at The Lodge.

She'd been to those parties before and never been caught.

But the one she borrowed the dress for and went to this term was nearly a disaster. She'd quarrelled with her boyfriend at the party and he'd gone off with someone else. Leaving her without a lift back to school. Then trouble had broken out, trouble that Miss Welbeck might get to hear about! Annie knew she had to get back to school quickly! She'd run to the phone box at the top of town and rung through to Parkinson, hoping to get hold of Pippa who would then come and fetch her in the car. But Miss Welbeck, of all people, had answered the phone!

Alerted by a phone call from Mrs Tarkus, who insisted that a Trebizon girl was involved in a fracas at a party in the town, the Principal had come hotfoot to the Upper Sixth boarding house intending to check and see if someone was missing.

Hearing Miss Welbeck's voice on the phone, Annie was panic-stricken!

She had to have a good testimonial from Miss Welbeck this term. Her whole future depended on it! In desperation, almost giggling with fear, she'd disguised her voice and pretended she was ringing from Court House - some Middle School kid - about to run away!

Anything to draw Miss Welbeck away from Parkinson. And it had worked!

Then, thank goodness, that empty taxi had come by and she'd grabbed it. The driver had prattled on to her about tennis, of all things, but she'd been much too fraught to bother about that!

She'd no idea he took her to be Rebecca Mason who only the previous evening had worn the very same outfit and been in the very same taxi.

The cab driver had been a good sport; he'd dropped her behind some trees and she'd threaded her way through them, silently on foot, just in time to see Miss Welbeck driving away from her private house, in the direction of Court! The coast was clear!

Five minutes later, she was home and dry, safely tucked up in bed.

Afterwards, it never occurred to her that she'd left the stole in the taxi. She was convinced she'd left it at The Lodge. She and Pippa had driven down there the next day, to try and recover it. But it had gone. It looked as though someone at the party must have pinched it.

'So Annie Lorrimer was the hoaxer! But what you haven't explained to us yet, Rebecca,' said Tish, 'is the business of the fire alert.'

It was Wednesday afternoon and they were all sunning themselves in the sand dunes, down in Trebizon Bay.

'I'm just coming to that,' said Rebecca. 'It's rather complicated.'

'Get on with it, then!' said Sue. 'We're all agog.'

'Well, you see. Miss Welbeck had seen Pippa's new dress, right at the beginning of term. She'd been over in Pippa's room, giving her some coaching. She'd admired it and Pippa had explained about me having exactly the same dress and how she wouldn't be able to wear it much.'

'Ah, Pippa is so sweet – yes?' said Mara.

'Very,' nodded Rebecca. 'Now the point is that when this Mrs Tarkus rang up and complained that night, *she described what the girl was wearing.* It sounded horribly like Pippa's dress to Miss Welbeck –'

'Or yours!' butted in Tish.

'Ah, but Rebecca's just Third Year, so it was Pippa she thought of first!' said Sue. 'That right, Rebecca? So she made a beeline for Parkinson, to try and find Pippa –?'

'Right,' nodded Rebecca. 'But then the funny phone call came through and so she forgot all about looking for Pippa that night. She nipped back home and got her car and came over to Court House instead. And when she got here, she was more interested in *me*, and the fact that I was wide awake and in my dressing gown, when I should have been fast asleep.'

'So it *could* have been you, at the party. Just got back!' exclaimed Margot.

Rebecca nodded.

'But the more Miss Welbeck thought about it, the more convinced she became that it wasn't me Mrs Tarkus saw. The hoax tied in too neatly. If *I'd* been to the party I'd hardly have wanted to draw her over to Court House. But if Pippa had been she'd have wanted to draw Miss Welbeck away from Parkinson!'

'Logical!' nodded Sue, eagerly. 'But you still haven't told us where the fire alarm fits in!'

'Give me a chance!' laughed Rebecca.

She picked up a handful of sand and let the grains run through her fingers. The other five were holding tight to their breath.

'For three horrible days Miss Welbeck thought it must be Pippa and waited for her to come and own up. She was terribly shocked and upset because she thought it was so out of character. Finally she called Pippa over to her study and accused her point-blank of going to the party. Pippa just flatly denied it and then –'

'What?'

'The fire alarm went off!'

They all gasped.

'Well, I'll be blowed!' exclaimed Tish. 'So Pippa was in with Miss Welbeck when that happened – and it was *Annie* I saw waiting downstairs! She knew Pippa was upstairs, at that very moment, getting the blame –'

'And she knew Pippa would never give her away!' put in Rebecca.

'So *she* did it?' said Tish. Expressively, she banged

her elbow into the sand. 'Bust the fire panel and set the bell ringing! A second hoax!'

'She'd been going through agonies!' said Rebecca. 'It was the only thing she could think of to put Pippa in the clear. And it worked! Miss Welbeck actually apologized to Pippa for misjudging her. After that Pippa should have been able to breathe a sigh of relief and forget the whole wretched business. But she couldn't. She just got more and more miserable . . .'

'Because Miss Welbeck stopped suspecting her, and started suspecting you, instead?' finished Mara. 'It was the only explanation left to her? You could have made that phone call, after all, even though it was a silly thing to do . . . after a party like that, you might have been silly enough for anything?'

'Yes,' agreed Rebecca.

'She as good as told Tish you were the culprit,' remembered Elf.

But Tish shook her head.

'No, I'm sure she didn't really mean it. I never got the feeling she *really* thought it was Rebecca. She was just playing some sort of game.'

'Oh, but she *did* really think it was me,' protested Rebecca. 'She told Pippa she did!'

'Ah!' exclaimed Tish, with sudden insight. 'And what could have been a better game to play than that?'

Tish was right. Miss Welbeck had suspected Pippa all along, not Rebecca. The only time she'd really wondered about Rebecca was immediately after the fire hoax. Pippa could hardly have been responsible for *that*!

But grilling Tish Anderson had removed any doubts about Rebecca – and it had also thrown up a clue. Tish had seen a senior girl near the fire alarm. One of Pippa's friends in the Upper Sixth, perhaps, trying to get her out of trouble?

If that were so, Miss Welbeck was sure she knew how to make Pippa confess. Let her see that young Rebecca Mason, a completely innocent person, was at some stage going to have to take the blame! Oh, yes, that should upset Pippa right enough . . . and it did!

But the expected confession had never come.

So Miss Welbeck was completely at a loss. Had Mrs Tarkus got the description of the dress all wrong? She'd got things wrong before. Was the timing of the two hoaxes just extraordinary

coincidence? Were they unconnected happenings . . .
two thoroughly stupid pranks, the second inspired
by the first, perhaps . . . now best forgotten?

And then, on Tuesday evening, Annie Lorrimer
had walked into her study and made a full confession.

The Principal simply couldn't get over it.

'The last person I would ever have suspected,'
she confided in Miss Gates later. 'Annie! So quiet.
A model pupil, all the way up the school. Hard
working, a dedicated musician, serious, sensible . . .'

'It's the quiet ones who sometimes break out in
the most unexpected ways, Madeleine. What on
earth are you going to do? Those master classes of
hers, in Japan. Will you write the testimonial she
needs?'

'I've already written it. It was posted a week ago.'

'Then –?'

'I shall rescind it, of course, Evelyn.'

Miss Gates was aghast.

'Must you? She wants this, more than anything
in the world! There's nothing else she wants out of
life, you know.'

'The evidence suggests otherwise,' commented
Miss Welbeck.

There was a heavy, contemplative silence.

Finally, Miss Gates asked –

'And Pippa? Will she be punished?'

'Whatever for?' said the principal. 'Hasn't she had enough punishment?'

She started to pour some coffee and at last her stern expression softened.

'I'm so completely and utterly relieved that the culprit wasn't Pippa,' she said.

She took her cup and crossed the room to a deep, comfortable chair by the open window. Summer scents from her garden wafted in.

'Let's hope we can settle down to the normal business of term now. I'll make an announcement about the summer camp this week – you know, the one Pegasus are going to run here. They've asked if any of our girls would like to stay on and help. Some of the children are quite small.'

With the abrupt change of subject the Principal had made her feelings clear. The matter of the hoaxes had been resolved and the chapter was now closed.

'I daresay there'll be no shortage of volunteers,' said Miss Gates.

FOURTEEN
Commemoration

It was hot, blisteringly hot. It was the last Saturday in June. It was Commem Day. In the morning the whole school had attended a special service in hall, to honour the person who had founded Trebizon, way back in the misty past. This evening, for Third Years and upwards, there would be the Commem Ball.

But now it was the afternoon and the final of the inter-schools cup was taking place. Trebizon *vs.* Helenbury. Trebizon had to win – they must! Rows of anxious faces, pressed against the wire netting all around south courts, were willing it – praying for it!

But Helenbury's two coachloads of supporters were cheering – cheering ecstatically! Trebizon's supporters were close to despair. They were groaning.

The umpire called out the score:

'Game to Helenbury. Helenbury lead five games to four in the final set.'

'Come on, Rebecca!' somebody called feebly. 'It's all up to you!'

In a blur Rebecca walked up to the umpire's chair and sank down on the bench beside it. Time for a break, thank goodness – time to change ends. She was gasping for breath as Miss Darling handed her a drink. Gazing around she realised in horror that all the other courts were empty now.

'We won two of the singles – and lost three.'

A shiver of tension ran through Rebecca.

'So it's four matches all and this is the decider!'

And Rebecca was 4–5 down in the final set!

No wonder Helenbury was cheering! No wonder Trebizon was subdued.

Because it was the cup final there were nine matches in all – three doubles and six singles. Trebizon had come out of the doubles section well – two matches to one. Poor Eddie Burton had tennis elbow: Pippa and Rebecca had been partners again! They'd hit top form together, especially the way they'd managed to outwit, between them, the giantess of the Helenbury team, a girl called Sophie

Smith. They'd defeated Sophie and her partner in two straight sets. Rebecca's five friends had cheered themselves hoarse during the match.

But now, in the singles section, Rebecca had to face Sophie alone. They were both ranked number five in their respective teams, so drawn against each other. What a match it was proving to be!

Sophie Smith was a big girl, with hitting power to match.

She'd taken a while to settle down and Rebecca had won the first set 6–4.

In the second set, Sophie had reversed that score, gradually beginning to grind Rebecca down with her strong service and powerful drives off the forehand and backhand.

Now, in the final set, each game had gone with service. But although the rallies were still long and exhausting, Sophie was gaining the upper hand, holding her service each time more convincingly than Rebecca was holding hers. And Rebecca was tired. So very, very tired!

If only it weren't so hot. If only the sun would go away!

'Take her service now, Sophie!' shouted a Helenbury supporter.

'*We want the cup!*' bayed the whole crowd of them. And then they started to chant it, over and over again.

Rebecca's legs felt rubbery as she stood up and arched her aching back. If she lost the next game, they'd have the cup all right! She felt hopeless. She hadn't anything left! Even if she held her service, she'd have to go on and break Sophie's and then still win the next game . . .

Then she heard Pippa's voice, clear and bell-like –

'Give us an "R" –'

'*R!*' roared the Trebizon crowd, drowning out everything else.

'Give us an "E" –'

'*E!*'

Rebecca walked up to the other end to begin serving. They were just finishing.

'– And who's going to win?' called Pippa.

'*REBECCA!*' came the deafening response.

And she did. 7–5.

Afterwards, Rebecca was mobbed. Miss Willis thumped her on the back. Pippa hugged her. Tish and Co rushed at her like excited labradors and nearly knocked her over. And Miss Darling definitely smiled at her! Then when Mrs Seabrook, the county tennis scout, presented the huge glittering silver cup to the Trebizon captain – Kate immediately thrust it into her arms!

'You have it, Rebecca!'

Rebecca was carried shoulder high off the court, holding the cup aloft. She was marched over to the now famous cedar tree and paraded round and round it like a lucky mascot until, laughing with joy and aching with tiredness, she begged to be put down. She leaned against its massive trunk for a few moments, drinking in the cool shade.

At the tennis tea, her opponent said, with a rueful smile:

'How you lifted your game like that, I'll just never know!'

Afterwards Mrs Seabrook drew her to one side.

'I'm going to see to it that you turn out for the county Under-14s before the summer's out!'

In that moment, Rebecca's pleasure reached new heights. *Thank you – Pippa!* She knew that Pippa's last memories of Trebizon would be less unhappy now. But to be at the receiving end of such unexpected and joyful news for herself was an added delight. A bonus!

The same afternoon, as Tish had predicted he would, Robbie won the Garth College tennis cup for the third year running. The stage was set for a very happy evening all round.

Rebecca looked lovely in the dress and stole. Everybody said so. It helped, because she suddenly felt shy and nervous when Robbie arrived to escort her to the Commem Ball. He was carrying some roses.

'This time the flowers really are for you,' he said, with a sheepish smile, remembering a past episode.

They both laughed.

And after that, everything was all right.

The Commem Ball had an atmosphere all its own. There were games with prizes as well as dancing to an excellent professional band. Outside it was still light; it was mid-summer and the sun set very late. Supper was served in the quadrangle gardens – all sorts of delicious savoury snacks and strawberries and cream to end up with. Then, in the balmy June dusk, a group came out to sing madrigals. Sue and Mara and Margot were amongst them – they'd been rehearsing for a month.

As she stood beside Robbie and listened to those sweet, Elizabethan songs, little shivers ran up and down Rebecca's spine, and a feeling of sadness, too. Pippa was leaving in the morning!

Towards the end of the evening, Pippa came up to her.

'There's a goodbye present for you over at the boarding house.'

'For me? What?'

Pippa just smiled mysteriously and put a finger to her lips.

'Your parents will probably like it,' she said and turned back to her partner.

Pippa was catching the early train to London. She'd be back at the end of term to collect her car and all her luggage and say her goodbyes. But now that the Upper Sixth had finished their exams there was nothing to keep them at Trebizon for the last three weeks of term. By tacit agreement, Annie Lorrimer had already gone, straight after exams. Tomorrow, Pippa was going to London and then Paris.

Her schooldays were just about over.

When Robbie took Rebecca back to Court House later he said goodnight to her and then she walked slowly inside. It had been the best day she could ever remember in her whole life.

'I must just see what Pippa's left for me,' she thought.

It was propped up in the hall, wrapped in brown paper, with her name on it. She pulled off the wrappings – and gasped.

'The painting!'

Rebecca stared and stared at it.

It was all there, the original canvas for the magazine cover, so painstakingly worked in oils. 'I love this tree!' Pippa had told her, on the first day of term. Rebecca gazed at the magnificent trunk with its massive girth – how real the bark looked! – and the layers of green on heavy boughs casting a deep, cool shade on the grass beneath. Beyond, peeping through, a glimpse of the old building, its mellow stone bathed in sunlight, soft and warm and luminous.

Rebecca looked at the tiny figure of herself. It could have been a stranger. A girl in white, come out of the hot sun and the red dust of battle on the tennis court, to fling herself joyously down on the grass . . . spreadeagled there beneath the cedar tree . . . held still forever.

Tomorrow Pippa would be on the train and it would be rushing along, faster and faster, saying *goodbye Trebizon . . . goodbye . . . goodbye . . .* over and over again.

'I love Trebizon,' Pippa had said to her, the day she finished the painting. 'In fact, I've been very happy here. This is how I'll always remember it. When I've gone.'

One day, Rebecca realised, she'd be going on that train, too.

She'd be only a memory, a small figure in a summer scene painted on canvas while Trebizon marched on.

'And this is how I'll always remember it, too,' decided Rebecca. 'When that day finally comes.'

But the day was still far off. She had a long time to go at Trebizon yet.

It was a happy thought.

Summer Camp at TREBIZON

Read about Elf's summer camp at **TREBIZON** in this special extract...

ONE
End of Term

'Please stop talking about the summer camp!' Rebecca Mason said to her friends, the day before school broke up. 'You know I can't stay on for it!'

It was the end of the summer term and their year in the Third at Trebizon was drawing to a close. In September, after the summer holidays, the six of them would be going up into the Fourth Year.

As if missing the summer camp weren't bad enough, Rebecca had other problems, too.

Her friends had all picked their Fourth Year options and knew exactly what subjects they'd be doing for the next two years, in preparation for their GCSEs at the end of the Fifth.

Rebecca still couldn't make her mind up and secretly she felt a little bit resentful that her parents were always so far away. Most of the Third had been able to keep in close touch with home over this question of Fourth Year options. Her two best friends, Tish Anderson and Sue Murdoch, had got themselves all sorted out. Tish wanted to be a doctor, like her father, and he'd advised her what subjects to concentrate on. Sue had got in a muddle but then her mother had been down over the Commemoration weekend and talked to some of the staff.

It was around then that Rebecca began to feel at a disadvantage, especially now Pippa had gone. The girl who'd just left the Upper Sixth would have given her so much good advice. But it was no good thinking about that.

Even Robbie Anderson, who might have been some help, was away on a French exchange.

Now term was almost over and Rebecca's parents were due home for two months.

Although she was longing to see them, that was a sore point, too. It was their fault she couldn't stay on for the summer camp! And there was the business of the dig in Mulberry Cove, as well . . .

Because they saw Rebecca so seldom her father and mother had planned these summer holidays in some detail, starting with a fortnight's tour of Scotland as soon as school broke up.

Rebecca's five friends were all staying on at Trebizon to help with a children's summer camp. Every single one of them was being allowed to stay on, even Mara Leonodis, whose father never used to allow her to do anything at all. For Rebecca, of course, it was out of the question. The holiday in Scotland had been planned for ages. She'd been excited about it until all these other things had come up. Now it was definitely marred.

'Please don't talk about it!' she repeated.

Lessons were over for the day and the six were on their way down to Trebizon Bay, cutting through the little wood at the back of Juniper House that led directly on to the sand dunes. It was here in the copse that the tents were going to be pitched on Friday.

The school governors were lending the campsite to the Pegasus Trust, an organisation that ran holiday schemes for city children who wouldn't otherwise have a holiday. Some were from very poor homes and others were in care. With a professional social worker in charge, all the voluntary help needed to run the camp and look after the children was being provided by the school. A lot of the Trebizon girls had volunteered, but there was only room for twenty. The five in Court House could hardly believe their luck when they were chosen.

They'd just been planning what games to organise for the children when Rebecca shut them up. Although Rebecca was really only teasing them they were overcome with remorse.

'Sorry!' said Tish in dismay.

'You know how much we're going to miss you, Rebecca!' wailed Elf – Sally Elphinstone.

'It's going to be rotten without you,' added Sue.

'Terrible!' echoed Margot Lawrence.

Mara said nothing. Although Rebecca was laughing by now the Greek girl knew better than anyone how she was feeling. Poor Rebecca!

They passed through the little gate marked TREBIZON SCHOOL PRIVATE that led directly on to Trebizon Bay. Rebecca and Tish ran on ahead and scrambled up to the top of the nearest sand dune. The huge bay was spread out in front of them with its great reaches of golden sand. The tide was a long way out today. Some little sailing boats, flashes of white on the green sea, were disappearing round the headland and into Mulberry Cove.

'When does Mrs Lazarus start her dig?' Rebecca suddenly asked Tish.

'Saturday, I think,' replied Tish.

'Do you think you'll be able to go and help, like she asked?'

'Only if we get any time off from the camp,' said Tish shiftily, trying to be casual.

'I think that sounds really interesting, I bet you'll go,' said Rebecca. 'And it *is* her last chance, after all.'

They'd all met Mrs Lottie Lazarus on the last Sunday in June. It had been Commemoration Day on the Saturday – a high point in Rebecca's life – and the Sunday had been Old Girls' day, when ex-Trebizonians of all ages descended. Sue's mother had been amongst them. In fine drizzle Rebecca had played in a School *vs* Old Girls tennis match and School had been trounced. Afterwards, at Court House, they'd entertained to tea some old Trebizonians who were visiting their former boarding house, including an elderly, scholarly lady with twinkling blue eyes in a sun-bronzed face and a charismatic personality.

Mrs Lazarus was easily the oldest 'old girl' Rebecca had ever met at Trebizon and she was fascinated by her. She'd been a leading expert in Latin literature all her life, but for the past two years had turned to archaeology, trying to prove a theory that no one really believed in. It was something to do with pirates in Roman times and a hoard of newly-minted Roman coins buried in Mulberry Cove, less than a mile from her old school.

'As soon as I read the text of the old poem, I knew it must be Mulberry Cove,' she told Rebecca, who had just brought her some sugar for her tea. 'I did no end of sailing round here at your age.'

She then quoted some very obscure Latin verse at Rebecca in order to convince her. 'You see!' Rebecca didn't see at all, but it sounded rather mysterious and exciting. She had seen a bulldozer in Mulberry Cove one day, shifting boulders. Apparently Mrs Lazarus had brought excavation parties down before.

'We're having our last dig next month, so I need plenty of extra help,' said Mrs Lazarus, who had taken a liking to Rebecca on sight. 'If you're staying on for this camp you and your friends can come over sometimes. You see –' she looked unhappy for a moment '– the people who gave me the grant are getting impatient.'

'I–I'm not staying on,' Rebecca had said, with

real regret. 'But I'm sure the others would like to help.'

Now as she stood on the sand dunes with Tish, gazing in the direction of Mulberry Cove, she was reminded of all this. She looked so wistful that Tish suddenly couldn't stand it any longer. She threw an arm round Rebecca's shoulders.

'I *wish* you could stay. Don't you sometimes wish parents had never been invented?'

When the telegram arrived, that was just what Rebecca wished.

Rebecca put the summer camp out of her mind and on Thursday morning she packed her big trunk feeling happy and excited. Her parents' plane was due in at Heathrow Airport at midday. They were hiring a car for the holidays and driving straight down to Trebizon to collect her. They'd all stop the night at a motel somewhere and by tomorrow night they'd be in the hilly Scottish borders!

There they were going to spend the weekend in Langholm, a pretty border town on the River Esk, with Nanny MacDonald, Rebecca's grandmother on her mother's side. And it was Rebecca's fourteenth birthday on Sunday! It would be wonderful to spend it with her parents and her Scottish Nan, who made delicious home-made baps and shortbread and Dundee cake. Rebecca's mouth watered at the thought of it. After that they were going to tour the Scottish Highlands, before returning to Langholm for the colourful Common Ridings and then back to their little house in London for the rest of the holidays.

Not that she'd be seeing a lot of London these holidays. She was booked to play in various tennis competitions during August and her parents would be taking her around to them. It would be interesting staying in different places.

She packed her things carefully, taking a last look at the painting Pippa had given her before wrapping it up carefully and placing it between layers of clothes in her trunk. She liked it more every time she looked at it and had decided to give it to her parents. Perhaps they'd hang it up in their apartment in Saudi Arabia and the sight of Rebecca in her tennis clothes beneath the big green cedar tree would remind them of England.

It was a hectic morning. All the beds in Court House were stripped and the rooms were being cleared out. The domestic staff was standing by ready to spring-clean the building from top to bottom. Rebecca and her friends and the other Third Years across the corridor were giving up their ground floor rooms and would be moving up to the first floor when they came back in September. Tish had gone out for a last training run because she was being taken to the County Sports after lunch and had set her heart on winning the 800 metres this year. But the other five rushed round saying their goodbyes and getting the school leavers' signatures in their autograph books.

The end of the summer term was always full of goodbyes. The Upper Sixth Formers were all leaving and had come back for end-of-term Assembly. Rebecca saw Pippa all too briefly and said goodbye to Della Thomas and Kate Hissup as well. There would be a new Senior Prefect and Head of Games in September.

The six friends had done well enough in the summer exams to stay in the A stream and so were going up *en bloc* from III Alpha to IV Alpha. Rebecca and Sue went and thanked Miss Hort for putting up with them for a whole year.

The III Alpha form mistress looked stern and mannish but she was great fun underneath. She wagged her finger at Rebecca, although her eyes were twinkling.

'Now remember what I've told you, Rebecca, and think about doing physics. You're good at chemistry and biology and your maths has shot up. I'm sure you're going to be a science person in the end.'

'But Miss Heath says I'm an arts person and should get on with some Latin now,' protested Rebecca. 'And they clash. I just don't know what to think!'

'Oh, yes, Latin,' said Miss Hort. She didn't look particularly approving. 'Well, you must sort it out with your parents. You're quite capable of doing either. Don't forget they're to write to Miss Welbeck in the holidays. Do you realise, Rebecca Mason, that you're the only girl left who hasn't sorted out her options?'

Rebecca grumbled to Sue about it afterwards.

'I wrote to my parents and they don't know any better than I do. I don't want to do physics – or Latin, either! I want to do home economics and scripture but they clash with chemistry and German and I like both of those. It's horrible having to choose, especially when they keep saying how important it is!'

'I know,' said Sue, sympathetically. 'It was a terrible headache fitting my GCSE music in. I'm just glad my mother came down for Commem.'

'I'm longing to see Mum and Dad!' Rebecca said suddenly.

But when they got back to the boarding house, several girls came running out.

'Mrs Barry's been looking for you everywhere, Rebecca!' shouted Aba Amori.

'There's been a telegram!' said Anne Finch. 'The postman came!'

'We wondered what the post van was doing here again!' added Jenny Brook-Hayes. They were all surrounding Rebecca. 'He's been once this morning.'

Mrs Barrington, the House Mistress, looked out of a window.

'Can you come round to my sitting room, Rebecca?' she called.

Sue walked round with her to the Barringtons' front door at the side of the building. As the House Mistress opened the door Rebecca stiffened a little and Sue gave her arm a squeeze. 'In you go, Rebeck. Hope everything's all right.'

Mrs Barrington led the way through to the sitting

room, waving a telegram.

'I'm afraid there's quite an upset. I've just had an overseas phone call as well. Your mother's been trying to contact me all morning. I've got all the instructions.'

'Has the plane been delayed?' Rebecca asked quickly.

'Worse than that – sit down a minute, Rebecca – I'm afraid your parents can't get back to England for another two weeks.'

'Two weeks!' exclaimed Rebecca in dismay. She subsided into a small armchair. 'Why, what's happened?'

Gently Mrs Barrington explained that Mr and Mrs Mason were still in Saudi Arabia, having had the first part of their summer leave cancelled because of an emergency at a desert installation. Mr Mason was needed urgently to supervise repairs and Mrs Mason, who was a trained nurse and had been working for the company since January, was also needed because some men may have been injured.

'Two weeks,' repeated Rebecca glumly. No trip to Scotland, after all! No birthday with her parents! 'Then, I – I'm to go to my grandma's on the coach, I suppose?'

Rebecca's other grandmother, who lived in Gloucestershire, was her official guardian in England when her parents were out of the country.

'No.' Mrs Barrington consulted some notes she'd made on a pad. 'You're to leave your trunk here and your parents will collect it in a fortnight's time, after they've collected you. You're to go to Bath. I've got the address.'

'Bath?'

'Yes, to your Great Aunt Ivy. It's an easy journey and it seems she's your only relative down south who's sure to be at home. She's not on the phone but your mother's sent her a telegram and presumably she's confirmed it because your mother says she'll be expecting you tonight.'

Rebecca's spirits sank even further. Great Aunt Ivy! She was well-meaning but a terrible fusspot and rather deaf as well, so you had to speak in a kind of a shout all the time. She was Gran's sister, but a lot older. Dully Rebecca remembered that it was round about now that Gran was going to visit her two sons in Canada, Uncle Bill and Uncle David, so obviously that was why she couldn't go to Gloucestershire. At least she knew a few people up there. She didn't know anyone in Bath. It would just be her and Great Aunt Ivy for a fortnight.

'All right, Rebecca?' asked Mrs Barrington, kindly. 'I'll sort out a good train for you this afternoon and give you the time of the connection.'

'Thanks,' said Rebecca, trying to summon up a smile. 'I'll just pack a small case, then, and leave most of my stuff here in my trunk.'

She felt like crying with disappointment. She also felt a kind of rage against her parents! Tish's comment from the day before came back to her.

Mrs Barrington drove her to the station some time after lunch.

In Rebecca's suitcase were several little packages in brightly coloured wrappings – birthday presents from the others, for her to open on Sunday. She wondered what kind of birthday she was going to have.

Tish had gone off to the County Sports and Rebecca's last glimpse of the other four was of them helping to unload the Pegasus camping equipment at the back of Juniper House. It had been sent on to the school by lorry in advance.

It was kind of the House Mistress to take her to the train, because she and Mr Barrington were themselves about to dash away on holiday. She bought Rebecca's ticket to Bath and put her on the right train. Rebecca thanked her.

But as she settled into her seat and the train drew away from Trebizon station tears welled up and she ground her teeth with rage. Tish was right. *Why had parents ever been invented?*

When she got to Great Aunt Ivy's house in Bath that evening, it was even worse. She stood her suitcase on the doorstep and knocked and knocked. The sound echoed up and down the quiet street, but no one came to the front door. Rebecca was rather taken aback. She knew her great aunt was hard of hearing, but surely she was expecting her?

She tried the door to see if it would open but it was firmly locked.

Then she noticed that all the windows were shut, some of them with curtains half-drawn across. She realised that she'd been wasting her time knocking.

There was nobody at home.